SALVATION

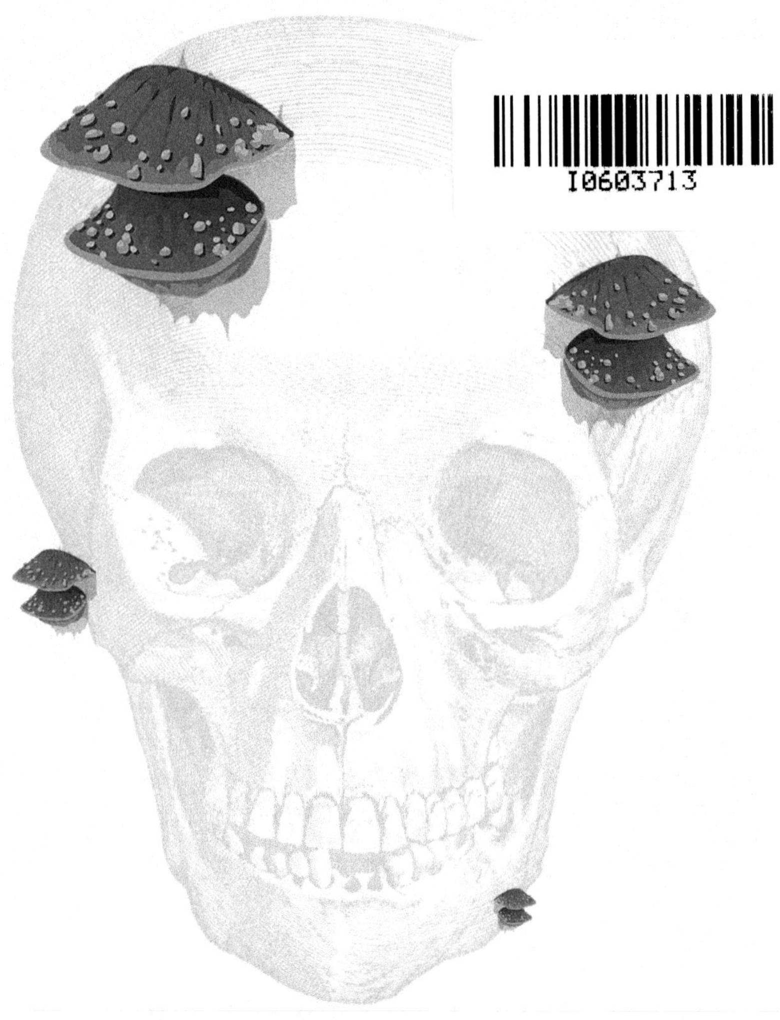

SPRING

ALSO BY T. C. PARKER

Saltblood

A Press of Feathers

Hummingbird

Maiden (with Ward Nerdlo)

The Long Con: An El Gardener Omnibus

THE EL GARDENER TRILOGY
The Debt (Book 1)
The Push (Book 2)
The Remembrance (Book 3)

SALVATION SPRING

TC PARKER

PUBLISHED BY NEFARIOUS BAT PRESS
2022

SALVATION SPRING
Second Paperback Edition

Published by Nefarious Bat Press

For E., W(ayne) & B(rad), who set this crazy train in motion

*And for *S., who kept it on the rails*

CHAPTER 1

She'd dreamed of the mines at Salvation Spring long before she ever saw them.

She couldn't have said for sure where the dreams had come from; what had planted the seed of them in the tired soil of her mind, those nights she closed her eyes and saw herself approaching the mountain. When the dust would crackle under her boots and the hot wind would burn through her lungs as she walked closer and closer to the hole torn out of the rock by older hands than hers, the hole she knew - but *couldn't* know - would lead her all the way down, if she'd only step inside.

Some days, when her head was cool and her thoughts came easy, she figured she must have overheard something that tipped her off to the town, the mines; picked up the thread of gossip at one of the bars she'd visited in Uriel or Halton or Sirach City and had the knowledge of the place sink, unbidden, into her bones. Other days, when her brain felt as cloudy as a mud-choked creek and those same thoughts slipped from her grasp like cutthroat trout no matter how hard she tried to cling to them, she was sure the dreams were visions: a gift from God, beamed into her through means she had no chance of ever understanding.

Either way, they'd come to her, *talked* to her, and she'd listened.

Sasha had woken from them, the first few times, with only the vaguest sense of where on the map Salvation Spring might be; of where she'd find the mines, if she went looking for them. But she'd asked questions and started conversations - with the blacksmith at Sirach City, the undertaker at Copper Forge, the cattlemen at Haarlem - and eventually she'd learned enough of the details to guide her there, if she was willing to cross the desert.

It took her weeks of travel, the crossing. Weeks of riding ten-hour stretches on the back of first the palomino Quarter Horse she'd acquired in Santa Catarina and then the tamed black Mustang she'd traded it for in Copper Forge, the one she'd nicknamed Puppy Dog after it came and nuzzled at her neck by the fire one night. Weeks of sleeping on a bedroll under a calfskin tent, those days and nights there were no towns or settlements or more comfortable accommodations in reach, while scorpions and camel spiders and the occasional rattlesnake crawled out from the stones and tunnels in the sand that kept them mostly hidden while the sun was out.

And then she was there - she and the Mustang walking slow-footed under the hanging sign bidding them *Welcome to Salvation Spring, Population 300*.

It was a dry, dead place, like so many of the towns and settlements she'd passed through before: a slice of cobbled path laid on baked-clay earth in the shadow of the hills above, the false-front procession of hastily erected stores and barber shops and boarding houses tailing off to shacks and cabins and a tin-roof chapel on the horizon. There was a funeral home, because there was *always* a funeral home, and a sheriff's office just next door, an empty set of three-man gallows mounted beside it.

Tufts of hair were caught up in the swaying hemp of the nooses, she realized as she drew closer: hair thick and thin, fresh and faded, woven in red and black and blond besides. An accidental tapestry of them; testament, most likely, to the unnecessary roughness of the executioner's grip.

She rode on, the Mustang's lope decelerating to a crawl.

There were no bodies at all on the thoroughfare: no drunks weaving unsteadily back and forth between the two saloons she could see, facing each other across the street; no ranchers bartering sides of beef for sacks of grain or delivering hides to the tannery; no old women in rocking chairs on the wide pine porch of the mercantile, making idle conversation over sweating jugs of iced water. Not a single, solitary one.

It was the heat, she thought. She could hardly stand it herself, and she'd almost had herself convinced she'd gotten used to it after so long in the desert, the brim of her hat pulled low over her eyes to block the unremitting glare of the light all around her - sweating the whole time through the bleached-brown duster that was all that kept her flesh from cooking in its skin. You couldn't stay out in it for long and keep your hold on reality as firm as you ought to; couldn't call yourself sane, when the rocks and deadwood blurred and twisted in the shimmer, threatening to turn to shapes no lucid soul could bear.

She drew the Mustang to a halt by the boarding house; tied him to the hitching post, stepped up to the entrance and knocked, the action sending a shock of pain through the raw knuckles of her heat-sore hands.

"She's not in there," said a voice behind her.

Sasha spun around quickly, the loose-fitting spurs in her heels carving shallow trenches in the parched earth under her feet.

He was lean, and long, and leathery brown - thin crow-black hair that was half grease and half sweet-smelling pomade reaching down to his shoulders, and a ragged salt-and-pepper beard obscuring a pock-marked face that could have been anywhere between forty and sixty.

His clothes were formal, as black as his hair: a frock coat over a buttoned vest and necktie, ironed dress pants and smart shoes polished to a high shine, in spite of the dust swirling gently around them. She knew him; knew his type, anyway. There was one like him in every town she'd ever stopped at. Couldn't *not* be.

"What *she*?" Sasha asked him. "The owner?"

"Ella-Mae," the man corrected her, sounding smoother than a man of his sepulchral looks had any right to. "Lady who runs the place. She's in church. Same as everyone else, this time of day."

He pointed a bony, hypermobile thumb over his shoulder, toward the makeshift chapel.

Sasha shrugged.

"Suppose I'll wait for her to come back, then."

"No point. All her rooms been taken up already. She's done accepting guests, even ones like yourself. *Ladies*," he clarified, with what she interpreted as a pointed once-over of her duster, her riding boots, the patched denim jeans hanging loose on her rangy, underfed frame.

"There anywhere else to stay in town?" she said, ignoring his stare.

"In the Spring? No. Ella-Mae's 'bout all we got."

Great, she thought - her back and thighs already beginning to ache at the prospect of another sleepless night on the bedroll, another sunrise waking to arachnid legs casting scuttling, kaleidoscopic shadows on the lightweight walls of her tent. *Perfect*.

"Come to think on it, though," he added, tugging ruminatively at the wispy, curling edges of his beard, "there *might* be somewhere, yet. You happen to pass a brick house on your way over, 'bout a mile south of here?"

She shook her head. There'd been nothing but sand and lumber and whitewashed clapboard between Salvation Spring and the last ghost town that Puppy Dog had led her through, she was sure of it. A brick house, a *real* house - something like that, she'd have remembered.

"It's not far," he said. "Not far at all."

"They got room?"

"*She*, not *they*. Another *she*. And I couldn't tell you, sorry. She's not a landlady, not like Ella-Mae. Just a doctor - or the nearest thing we got to one in the Spring, anyhow. But she's got a spare bed she's been known to open up to travelers, from time to time."

"You know what she charges?" Sasha said - conscious of her almost-empty money belt, of the handful of gold coins that were all she had left to trade.

"Not a clue," he replied. "Not a goddamn clue. Why don't you head on out there and ask her? Say old Rooster sent you."

"Rooster?"

If it was a nickname, she thought, then she couldn't so much as hazard a guess as its origins. There was something avian about the man, sure enough, with his hunched-over posture and his craning neck - but he should've been a Nighthawk, or maybe a Vulture. Not a farm-bird; not a *Rooster*.

"Yeah." He flashed her a grin, his teeth the shape and color of the coffins she could imagine him assembling for his customers. "Don't you worry. She'll know *just* who you mean."

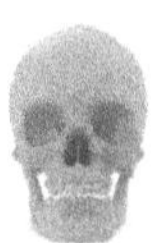

It was a pretty house, unnaturally pretty: the reddish brickwork and rectangular proportions of the building reminding her a little of the brownstones she'd known back east, a very long time ago, and nothing at all of the bleached timber that had come to dominate the west. There was picket-fencing all around it - sharp-edged stakes painted red and white as Christmas candy canes, demarcating the orderliness of the plot from the dehydrated wilderness it had sprung from. Lace curtains in the windows, pulled respectably shut; a wreath of cacti above the door handle.

And a garden. A *garden*, for God's sake: a lush carpet of green grass and pink dahlias and red poinsettias, so improbable in the middle of the desert that it might have been a *trompe-l'oeil* painted directly onto the landscape.

Conscious of her knuckles, she knocked more tentatively than she had at Ella-Mae's door. When no-one answered, she tried again - eschewing her fist for the bony tip of her elbow, the noise it generated as she drove it into the hardwood enough, she thought, to wake the dead.

"Jesus, Rooster!" she heard a woman's voice call out from inside - urgent, a little panicked even. "Come *in*! What're you waiting for, a written invitation?"

She thinks I'm him, Sasha thought. *The undertaker from the Spring.*

But maybe that's a good thing, if it gets me in the house?

She pushed at the door with a flattened palm; it opened easily under her hand, swinging inward to reveal the single, very large room within.

She saw a double bed, topped by a patterned quilt decorated with interlocking geometric shapes she recognized but couldn't place; a wool tapestry above it, faded to indecipherability; a log fire, flames licking at the base of the cast-iron cooking pot it heated and what looked like a gallon of water bubbling inside.

A solid oak table, big enough for twelve apostles. A girl splayed out across it, screaming, her dress hitched up to her waist. And standing between her legs a woman, blond-haired and covered with blood, her hands and forearms so doused with it that she could have been wearing gloves.

She turned her head Sasha's way, at the sound of the door opening - keeping her red-stained hands, Sasha noticed, exactly where they were, between the screaming girl's legs.

"You're not Rooster," she said. Surprisingly calmly, Sasha thought, in light of her predicament.

"No," Sasha answered - eyes drawn inexorably to the girl on the table, the blood pooling around her lower body and seeping into the wood below, and ears aching from her screams.

"You got clean hands?" the woman asked.

Sasha glanced down at her palms; at the dirt caked into the lines and creases there.

"No," she said.

"Then wash them - now. There's hot water in the bucket by the fireplace."

"I don't...," Sasha started, half paralyzed with shock.

"*Right now*, please," the woman repeated, more firmly. "This can't wait."

In a daze, Sasha obeyed: walked across to the fire, found the bucket, picked up the scouring brush beside it, plunged her hands into the water up to the wrists and scrubbed, until the mud and dust and soot were gone.

"What now?" she said, looking automatically to the woman for instruction.

"Come over here," the woman told her, beckoning Sasha with a bloody index finger.

Again, Sasha acquiesced, though not without trepidation. The girl's blood was singing in her nostrils now; the ferrous poison of it dancing in her throat and on the tip of her tongue, so intense she could taste it. It was jarring, intoxicating; something like seasickness, and something like the sick disorientation she occasionally felt with six shots of white whiskey in her gut.

Up close, the situation was clearer. The girl, she saw, was pregnant, her belly bulging under the fabric of her dress; pregnant, and deep in the throes of labor. There were small tools laid out on the table, by her ankles. *Surgical* tools: sharp scissors, a scalpel, a clamp and threaded needle.

One of the blond woman's hands, she also saw, was *inside* the girl - reaching for something it seemed it couldn't quite grasp. The other hand was clasped around the handle of another kind of surgical implement: a pair of silver tongs, themselves buried an inch or so in the girl's womb, and apparently holding it open.

Forceps, Sasha thought. *They're called forceps.*

"Baby's stuck," the woman said. "I'm gonna need to pull him out. So I'm gonna need *you* to hold *these*," she indicated the forceps, "just like *this*, like I am, so I can get to him. Think you can do that?"

Sasha nodded. And then the forceps were in her hands, and the *woman's* hands were inside the girl, and *then* - in what felt like a matter of seconds - the woman was cradling a baby, naked and bloody and crying for air.

"Can you cut that?" the woman asked Sasha, gesturing this time to the umbilical cord still connecting the infant to its mother.

"Yes," Sasha replied. She withdrew the forceps - slowly, very slowly - from inside the girl, and picked up the scissors from the table; took them in both hands, as if she were cutting a ribbon, and slid the blades over the cord. It was tough, springy as thick elastic, but it yielded to pressure. Without thinking, and without really understanding how she even knew to do it, she grabbed the clamp; unclipped it, and secured it to the remaining inch of cord that dangled from the place the baby's navel would eventually be.

"Good job," said the woman approvingly. She drew a length of cotton sheet from the pocket of her pants - *men's* pants, Sasha noted, just like her own - and wrapped the infant up in it. "Hold him?" she added. "While I see to *her*?"

Sasha didn't answer - because what was there to say? - but she took the baby, feeling its tiny body writhe hotly in the clean but now bloody palms of her hands.

Only then did she look up at the girl on the table - who was, she saw now, very, *very* still. Not moving at all, in fact: her eyes closed and her chest neither rising nor falling. Blood and a darker, more gelatinous gore still trickled down her thighs from her uterus - but slowly, hesitantly, like the final drops wrung from a near-on empty liquor barrel.

She's dead, Sasha thought. *We got the boy in time, but not the mother.*

The blond woman stepped around the table to the place where the girl's head rested, her matted brown hair pressed against a sweat-stained pillow someone - Sasha figured the woman - had slipped under it.

Leaning in, her own head and shoulders bending into the girl's motionless upper body, the woman brushed the girl's temple with her lips. She breathed in deeply through her nostrils, exhaled, and placed three more brief, tender kisses on the girl's face: on the cheek, the forehead, and finally the lips.

And the girl's eyes, to Sasha's very great surprise, began to open.

CHAPTER 2

Y ou want to go to the mines?" the blond woman asked Sasha - her tone
pitched somewhere between disapproval and incredulity. "You sure
about that?"

She looked different now, to Sasha at least; now the blood had been
washed from her face and hands and she'd exchanged her ruined pants and
shirt for a cleaner gingham dress. Younger - less the hardened battlefield
medic, and more a woman very close to Sasha's own age, somewhere in her
middle thirties. And healthy, too: not skin and bones and sunburn, the way
that Sasha was - the way the desert had made her - but rounder, *fuller*. Like she
had enough to feed herself, when she needed to; like she'd never had to eat a
yucca plant raw, straight out of the ground, or suck the fluid from a prickly
pear to keep her mouth from drying.

Her name was Jess, she'd told Sasha; Jess Aken. And she wasn't a doctor,
whatever Sasha might have heard.

"I know a little about drugs, and a little about surgery," she'd said,
declining to expound on how she'd come upon the knowledge. "And I grow a
few things, in the garden out front. Word gets around, and suddenly I'm the
town medicine woman. Trust Rooster to play along with *that* notion."

Under ordinary circumstances, Sasha might have asked her about her relationship with Rooster: how they'd come to know one another, and why - more importantly - Jess had leapt to the conclusion that it was Rooster and not Sasha who'd walked through her door the day before.

After what she'd seen, though - and what she thought she'd seen Jess *do* - she had other, more burning questions. Specifically, about the girl on the table. The table they'd *at that moment* been sitting down at, sipping cold sweet tea from the pitcher Jess had set down on the pure-white tablecloth that by then had covered the blood-spattered oak; the girl Sasha had seen with her own eyes *come back* from wherever she'd been, after Jess had kissed her.

Not *just* come back, either. Sasha had seen the girl sit up on her elbows; take her little boy in her arms and put him to her breast to feed while Jess had stitched her up. And then, before the sun had even set, seen her *get up and leave the house altogether*, albeit unsteadily and wincing with every step between the table and the door - taking off for town in the back of her startled husband's cart, her new-born son still clasped against her chest.

"What you did, earlier...," Sasha had begun, but Jess had interrupted her.

"You're looking for a place to stay," she'd said, matter-of-factly.

"What?" Sasha had replied, wondering how in the hell the woman had *known*. "I mean... yeah. I guess."

"It's three dollars a week, breakfast included. The bed'll be set up over there in the corner, across from mine, so don't expect a lot of privacy. And I'll probably ask you to help out in the garden, if you stick around long enough. That work for you?"

Sasha had thought of the coins in her money belt, the barely five dollars they amounted to; then of toast and eggs and coffee in the morning, and a stomach that didn't hurt at night from hunger. And she'd agreed.

"Alright, then," Jess had said. "Now that's settled. What brings you all the way out to the Spring?"

Sasha had weighed up how to frame it; how to explain why she'd come and what she was planning on doing, when she wasn't even sure she understood herself.

In the end, she'd settled on the basic facts, but not the rationale: that she was looking for something, and she thought she might find it in the mountains, down in the mines.

Jess had been horrified.

"You're *sure* you're sure?" she repeated now. "The mines... I wouldn't exactly call them *safe*. There've been more'n a couple of... *incidents*, I guess you'd say. Out there in the desert."

She ought to ask her why, Sasha knew: *why* the mines weren't safe, what kind of *incidents* there'd been. But she didn't.

Because you don't want her to tell you, she thought. *You don't want to know. Or maybe you're afraid you know some of it already, the same way you knew about the mine at all. That it's buried in you, somewhere - the knowledge.*

"I'm sure," she said.

"You mind if I ask *why* it is you want to go there? There's no gold in those mountains, if that's what you're looking for; never has been. No silver, either. It's never been clear just how there came to *be* mines there at all, tell you the truth. Since there's nothing there to mine."

Sasha shifted in her seat, uneasy.

"It's complicated," she said. And there it was again: the scene that haunted her, that had *been* haunting her what felt like forever. The empty signifier, the image without a referent. The memory, if that was what it was.

Hands on her, all over her. Not two but many, a dozen or more, the feel of them like cinders against the cold of her skin. Probing.

Pitch black above her, shards of luminescence puncturing the dark. Not stars, though; they couldn't be stars.

Pain. So much pain, and everywhere: as if every muscle and bone were tearing, every joint and fiber stretching somewhere beyond the point of endurance.

Her head thick but sharp, burning; a hot metal spike of agony driven through fog and molasses.

Chanting: the same mantra, again and again, in a language that seemed to her to be barely speech at all.

And the sense - the certainty - of something solidifying in the darkness. Something becoming.

"Complicated?" Jess said.

She won't let it go, Sasha thought. *She'll keep right on asking, until I give her something.*

"I had... an accident, I guess," she said, hoping the words she chose carried enough of a ring of truth that the other woman would believe her; would let the subject drop. "A while ago now. I don't recall much of what happened. I sort of... lost time, I think. Before and after. And when I woke up, I was... somewhere else. Up north." She wavered. "But I think maybe this town, the mines... that they're something to do with it. With how I got... hurt."

The first thing she'd felt, coming to, was the cold: ice wind blowing all around her, piercing the furs that had been draped, somehow, around her neck and shoulders. Then the ache, across her skin and under it: the deep, itching soreness of broken things healing, of ripped and ruptured things knitting together not quite the way they'd been before.

She'd thought of her mother: of raised voices, and slamming doors, and instructions to *just go, before you make it worse.* Of stepping outside into warm night air, footsteps following just behind her.

But between her mother and the cold, the brokenness and the wholeness she'd been sure must have preceded it, there'd been no recollection at all: nothing but void, smooth and seamless and indecipherable. An edgeless lesion on the surface of her memory.

Only later had the *other* fragments come, in flashes and sensations: the hands, the pain, the chanting.

In sights she had no right to be seeing; sounds she had no right to be registering.

"And you think going down to the mines is gonna help you piece it back together?" Jess asked her, curious now. "Trigger something, maybe? Get you remembering what happened?"

Sasha shrugged, a noncommittal gesture that was neither agreement nor dissent - afraid that even the smallest dip of the head or blink of the eye would give away more than she had already.

"I don't know," she answered. "Maybe."

Jess reached across the table for the pitcher, her bare wrist brushing Sasha's duster-covered arm as it passed her.

"I'd tell you to be careful," she said, pouring herself a second glass and adding an inch or two of tea to Sasha's, "but I got a feeling you wouldn't listen. And call me a mind-reader, but I got *another* feeling you don't wanna hear me tell you *why* you ought to be careful. That about right?"

Sasha didn't reply; didn't look up from her glass.

"Now normally," Jess went on, "I wouldn't push. What folks do or don't do with their bodies, what they decide what thing they do or they don't wanna know about... that's their business, not mine, and I try to respect their wishes. But the mines, those mountains up there... I don't believe I could live with myself, if I didn't tell you some of what I know about them. What I've heard, and what I've seen with my own two eyes. So you can hate me after for telling you, if that's what you have to do. That's out of my hands. Right now, though, I'm gonna need you to listen up, alright? Just sit right there, and *listen*."

CHAPTER 3

The body was still warm, she said, the first time the Sheriff called her out to the desert: cooked in its juices by the sun, but fresh, too. Barely dead at all.

She'd known who he was - who he'd *been* - by sight, though she was sure they'd never had a conversation extending much beyond polite greetings and small-talk reflections on the state of the weather. He'd never brought a gut ache or a sprained ankle or a rotten tooth to her door, the way that some of the men from the Spring had; had never approached her on the street, hat in his hands and a sheepish look in his eye, to ask her for a bottle of the special licorice medicine he'd heard she'd been able to rustle up for some of the other fellas in town, when they needed a little pick-me-up.

He'd been a day laborer, or so she'd thought: one of the hard-faced, interchangeable handful who picked up whatever odd jobs were going when the ranches and the sawmills were busy. And then, or so she'd figured from the state of his body, he'd served a very different purpose, for somebody.

His arms and legs had been dislocated: wrenched loose from the sockets at his hips and shoulders and hanging, limp as a marionette's, from the connective tissue that still held them in place, as if he'd been tied to wild horses that had dragged him toward the four points of the compass but given up just before they'd finished the job. The skin of his chin, neck and bare chest had been flayed and shredded, she'd assumed from his having been pulled face-down along the ground; blood had seeped through his pants and then dried there, stiffening to a deep red crust on the light blue denim.

And there'd been more; more, and worse.

There'd been insects and arachnids, a carpet of them, *on* him and *in* him. Black widows and furred tarantulas crawling over one another across his face and torso, their bristly legs poking, exploratory, from his open mouth and nipping curiously at the raw exposed flesh of his stomach. Giant centipedes and scarab beetles, swarming from his ears and nostrils and marching in erratic, crisscross patterns across his face and hair and scalp. Paper wasps and blowflies, dancing on and off the flesh wounds at his throat and forehead and the bare, scraped remains of his biceps - their low, atonal buzzing all but masking the murmured rustling of the desert wind.

She'd asked the Sheriff what had happened - if he knew. He'd shaken his head *no*; looked down at the laborer's body and grimaced, the twist of his lips and wrinkle of his nose suggesting he was somewhere close to losing his lunch.

"He'd choked to death," she told Sasha, helping herself to yet another glass of the sweet iced tea. "Suffocated on the... things in his throat. The insects. We cleaned them off of him with water, the ones we could see, then took what was left of him on over to Rooster's office - he's got a mortician's table in there, better equipment than I do out here. Rooster wasn't happy about it, not one bit, but he let us in, and the three of us got the body up on the slab and cut on into it. And what was in there..."

"What?" Sasha said, her own stomach turning.

"Bugs. About as many inside of him as there'd been outside: spiders and ants and crickets and I don't even *know* what else, squirming around in his belly and creeping on up into his throat. Looked just about like someone had made a hairball out of legs and shells and shoved them all the way down his gullet."

"Jesus." Sasha's gorge rose, something acrid burning in the back of her own throat at even the thought of the man's body cut open on the slab, insects pouring from his guts onto the sawdust floor.

"*How* they'd come to be in there… well, I'm not sure any one of us had the first idea, and we've seen some things between us, me and Rooster. Something that like… you just don't *get* that, not on a body that fresh. I don't even know that you'd see it on a body that's been a month in the ground."

The Sheriff had written down some of what he'd seen, and some of what Jess and Rooster had told him, about heat and decomposition and insect activity; tucked his notebook and the little pencil stub he carried with him back into the top pocket of his vest, and - still green about the gills - excused himself, leaving Rooster to take care of what was left of the corpse and the things that had spilled out of it.

Exactly a week later, he'd called her back out to the same stretch of desert - sending the request via his Deputy, a worried-looking redheaded kid so nervous he could barely get the words out when she'd opened the door to ask him what he wanted.

The second body had belonged to a man she hadn't recognized at all: a stranger, not someone from the Spring or any of the other towns or settlements nearby. He was young, or so she'd surmised barely old enough to drink. And the condition he'd been left in had caused a brief thunderclap of nausea to ripple through even *her* normally iron-clad constitution.

His face had been torn off - the skin of it hanging from behind his ears in bloody scraps like a discarded mask and separated from the tissues below not cleanly, as with a knife or some other sharp implement, but raggedly, as if by the claws of a wild animal or a whirling of blades caught up in a hurricane.

He'd been naked, unlike the first man, his pants and underwear missing as well as his shirt - giving her, the Sheriff and the horrified boy-Deputy the fullest possible picture of the damage that had been done to him.

Though his limbs had been dislocated, like the first man's, one of his legs had been missing altogether - leaving nothing but a bloody hollow where the bone and cartilage ought to have been. Strips of shredded skin had dangled in ribbons from his ribs, his thighs, the side of his neck.

And the insects – there were more of them, and worse than before, an infestation of spiders and roaches and desert-bugs defying description, worrying at his lips and eyeballs and belly button and burrowing in and out of the tiny holes and furrows hacked out of his midsection. What skin he'd had left on his body had pulsated with them – critters oscillating up and down in fluttering fibrillations so regular they could have been moving to the beat of his heart.

"Go get Rooster," she'd told the Sheriff. "Get him to bring his wagon out here - the one with the lid that locks. We're gonna need it."

The Sheriff, the smell of the vomit he'd evidently unloaded before she'd got there still clinging to him, had thrown her a brief salute of understanding and climbed - more shook-up than she'd ever known him be - onto the back of his buckskin, heading back toward town and leaving her and the Deputy to stand watch over the body.

She'd worried that, left out there with the bugs in the glare of the midday sun, the boy might take ill - come down with sickness or a fainting spell that'd leave her having to treat *him*, before she could even start in on examining the corpse. But he'd surprised her: had stood tall and back straight even in the crippling heat, with only the wrinkling of his nostrils betraying the queasiness she'd been sure he was fighting.

"You alright over there?" she'd asked him.

"Are *you*?" he'd replied - pretty reasonably, she'd considered, under the circumstances.

"I just meant, it's not usual, something like this. I don't expect you've seen much like this before, 'round the Spring. So no-one'd blame you for feeling sick about it."

He'd turned to look at her, sharply, a queer sort of fire in his wide green eyes.

"It might not be *usual*," he'd said, "but it ain't *new*. Not altogether."

She'd asked him what he'd meant by that.

"Those things on him. The critters." He'd pointed down at the dead man, at the insects making a banquet of his hole-ridden skin. "It's happened before. Right here in the desert."

"When?" she'd said. She'd been in the Spring a long time, more years than the Deputy had lived, and she'd never seen anything like it; never *heard* of anything like it.

"Long time ago, ma'am. Long time." He'd cupped a hand to his face, shielding his nose and mouth from the warm-carrion stink of the body drifting over on the breeze. "Before I was born. Before my *daddy* was born, even. Back when my gramma was young."

"Go on."

The boy had looked away from the body; cast a glance up to the mines and to the deadwood, orange-dust hills above them, both drenched in a sunlight so deep and permeating that they might have been painted on the dry-powder landscape in blood.

"She talked to me 'bout it, 'fore she passed," he'd begun. "Sort of... chiding me, you know? Warning me off coming here, to the desert. Said there were bad things gone on out here, things she'd never want me knowing."

"Things like *this*?" Jess had pressed him, the force of her question impelling him to turn back to the dead, excoriated man still crawling with bugs in the dirt.

"Yes, ma'am. Just *exactly* like this, the way she told it."

Jess had considered the words, the meaning behind them.

"How old are you, Deputy?" she'd said.

"Seventeen this last August, ma'am."

"And your gramma? How old is *she*?"

For all his nervousness, the boy hadn't been dumb, not dumb at all, and he'd caught on quick enough to what she was *really* asking him.

"Can't say I know exactly, ma'am," he'd told her, fixing the green of those eyes on *her*. "Ain't the sort of thing you ask an old lady, is it? But if you want to know how long ago they happened, those things she took to telling me about… I'd say we're looking at fifty years, easy. Longer, maybe."

CHAPTER 4

Jess hadn't liked it; not one bit. But *not* going out to the hills, to the mines, after traveling so far for so long... it wasn't an option for Sasha. Not even after the stories Jess had told her, she figured to deter her; not even with the specter of the writhing, bug-infested bodies that had lain there hanging over the place.

When Jess had reluctantly traced out a bare-bones sketch of a map for her to follow, if for no other reason than to stop Sasha getting lost among the endless fall and rise of pitted-orange earth, and when the Mustang was saddled, she lit off north, for the crags of hilltop in the distance.

She skirted the loose perimeter of the Spring, set on avoiding getting caught up in the town limits and having to explain herself to the locals or to Rooster the undertaker - and, even with the Mustang moving at a pace so sedate it was practically regal, was in spitting distance of the mines by noon, sun-sweat pooling at her neck and soaking through the short black strands of her hair below her hat.

The first of the mine entrances she came to was boarded, thick planks nailed across the rugged hole in the red rock and nothing but darkness visible through the cracks. The second was more promising: the hole there half-blocked by fallen stones and piled wood, but with enough space left between the almost-roof and the stones for her to crawl through.

There were no railroad tracks, she noticed; no wagonways, no means by which a mine cart might transport coal or ore, or whatever else was down there, out from under the ground into the open air. They must have been removed, she figured; the rails and sleepers and nails pulled out from the dirt when the mines shut down, whenever the hell *that* had been.

A hot, grit-filled cloud of dust blew past them, what felt like out of nowhere, and Puppy Dog - usually so calm, so stoic - reared up, damn near throwing her out of her saddle. She stayed upright, just about, even with sand tearing up her eyes - but when she rubbed at them, ground a knuckle in to wipe away the grit, another flash of something began to take shape at the edges of her vision.

It was familiar; all too familiar. It had come to her before: at cheap hotels in Boone and Hardknott; on the floor of the general store at Cooper Bridge; pitching her tent on the grasslands between Aurora and Obsidian. Never quite fully formed, never entirely *there*; always visible to her, but not to those around her. Not to the bartenders or the store-owners or the dice-rolling gamblers whose faces she'd looked into for confirmation that she was seeing what she *thought* she was seeing, but who'd done nothing but look back at her blankly, confused by her sudden attention; not to the purebred Arabian she'd been traveling with on the plains, who hadn't so much as twitched a muscle, even with the... thing standing so close it could've reached out a hand to touch the animal's tail.

It was a ghost, she figured - a ghost, or a hallucination. One that followed her around; one that only *she* could see.

And always the *same* ghost, everywhere.

It was small: shorter than her, perhaps the height of a twelve-year-old child, and slight, the bone of its hunched shoulders visible through the thin brown robe that covered it from head to toe. What skin she could discern through its hood was white: the sickly fish-belly white of a grub, something starved too long of natural light. There were sores across the surface of the skin, not red but green, clustered on its cheeks and arms in irregular patterns that reminded her of mold spores, of the mottled cap of a fruiting fungus - almost, as she'd thought from the very first time she'd seen it, as if it was rotting.

Its eyes were black: entirely black, the inky carbon of a deep-sea shark or a barracuda. Always black, and always watching her.

It's in your head, she told herself. *That's all it ever is - in your head. Ignore it. Move on.*

She looked away from the ghost - the hallucination - and flicked her own eyes instead back to the stone-blocked hole leading down to the mine.

And the smell hit her: so hard, it was a wonder she'd been able to miss it before. It was rancid, fleshy: a waft of spoiled meat and rot, and under it the flavor of something rank fermenting, of stomach gases mixing and stewing in the desert air.

She craned her neck in the direction it seemed the smell was coming from, somewhere to her left.

And saw the hand, fingers stretched out in the dust like they were grabbing for something; the wrist leading up to what must have been the accompanying body, hidden behind a boulder.

She considered leaving, there and then: riding back to Jess' place, filling Jess in on what she'd seen - what she *thought* she'd seen - and leaving it to her and the Sheriff to pick up the pieces. But it was a coward's way out; she knew it and, knowing it, couldn't quite bring herself to actually go ahead and *do* it.

The Mustang reared again, less violently - reacting, she thought, to the odor of death as much as to the dust-cloud. She ran a damp palm over his mane to calm him, as gently and soothingly as she felt able to; then, rallying what few reserves of courage she had left, guided him over to the boulder, to the place where she knew the body was waiting.

If you could still call it a body.

It had been young, male, shirtless - very much like the other ones Jess had described. It might even have been pretty once, though it was impossible to say now, with so much of its face gone, so many of its features torn away.

There were insects, on it and in it and over it: the same hovering bugs and crawling worms and fat-bodied spiders streaming like vomit from the remains of its mouth, like loosened coils of intestines from the holes in its stomach cavity.

Insects, but not *only* insects.

Sprouting upward and four inches into the dry air from the dead kid's orbital sockets, through the vitreous body of what used to be his eyeballs, were the thin greyish stalks of two separate clumps of mushrooms: Enoki mushrooms, Sasha thought they might have been called. Another clump hung down from one side of his lips like an exploded cigar; a third rose from his belly button with the faded grandeur of a wilting erection.

And from his chest, growing out from the gaping wound it had left in his breastbone, a flower: an orchid the size, shape and color of a pomegranate, its white leaves spread open to reveal a circle of seeds inside as square and red as a set of bloody teeth.

CHAPTER 5

t surprised her how calming she found it, watching Jess cook: seeing her tear roughly at the leaves and stalks of the greens she pulled from the garden, chop beets and squash and pumpkin into eighths and quarters on the tabletop, or add beans and sunflower seeds to a stew-pot bubbling with onions and tomatoes, or grind acorns into flour to make bread. There was a kind of care to the ritual; an affection and a tenderness Sasha had never had prior cause to associate with food or the preparing of it, but which seemed, somewhat oddly, to soothe her, whenever she was around to observe it.

"You don't eat meat?" she asked Jess one afternoon, when it had finally struck her what was missing in the meals she'd been eating, what Jess hadn't been putting in the stew-pots or leaving to slow-fry on the skillet.

"Never have." Jess pulled out a chair and sat down beside her at the table, the thick lentil soup she'd made for them spilling out from the sides of her bowl and Sasha's as she set them to rest on the placemats. "Can't say I had much of a taste for it to begin with, and now... well, I guess I've seen enough dead flesh to turn me off it altogether, you know?"

Sasha knew. It'd been a week since she'd set out for the mines, a week since she'd uncovered the dead boy's body and torn back to the Spring at a gallop to tell Jess and the Sheriff and Rooster the undertaker and whoever the hell else needed to know about what she'd found - and the prospect of cutting a knife through bleeding steak or chewing through sun-dried jerky with the consistency of weathered skin had never held less appeal.

Jess had been nothing but kind to her, in the aftermath of the discovery. Feeding the two of them without ever asking Sasha if she needed feeding; checking in on Sasha's state of mind, on the way Sasha was handling what she'd seen out in the desert, even as she and Rooster and the Sheriff had set to the business of finding out what in God's name had actually happened to the boy with the stalks in his eyes and the flower growing out of his chest.

Though what she'd found out so far - if she'd found out anything - she'd kept very much to herself.

She *had* however insisted, more vociferously even than she had the first time around, that Sasha stay away from the mines, at the very least until they could be sure that going there was... if not safe, exactly, then not likely to place Sasha in any immediate jeopardy. And Sasha had objected, though with nothing like the conviction of before, but had been secretly a little glad, in the end, to capitulate - giving Jess her word that she'd stay right there, in the Spring and ideally on Jess' land, until at least *some* idea could be had of who was going around turning healthy young men into what amounted to worm-food and fertilizer. What she'd seen at the mines had scared her, scared her badly - the apparition in its hood as much as the dead boy and his injuries. And maybe, or so she'd told herself, she could afford to cut herself a little slack. Could hold off going back out there for a week or two.

She *needed* to go, she knew that. But maybe she didn't need to go right away, after all. Maybe whatever was out there, *down* there - and whatever it might tell her - could stand to wait a while.

Besides: being around Jess had turned out kind of pleasant, in itself.

In the spirit of making herself useful, of giving herself something to do besides sit around and turn over images in her head, she'd offered to help out with some of the services Jess performed for the people in town, and outside of it: the healing and the herbs and the occasional setting of a bone or stitching of a wound. The trickle of patients had been slow but steady: three or four of them a day, every day, knocking gingerly at the door to the house in search of something for the pain in their leg, the slice across their palm, the on-again off-again throbbing behind their temples. None especially demanding, and not one of them in anything like as bad a way as the girl with the baby caught up inside her, but enough for Sasha to feel like she was doing something and not just standing around like a spare part: fetching hot water and threading clean needles and holding cuts closed while Jess sterilized gashes and applied ointments to bruises and measured out six doses of this medicine or that into one of the clear brown bottles she kept inside her store cupboard by the window.

There'd been no repeat of the magic trick Sasha was sure she'd seen that first visit: no strange, loaded kisses to the forehead, no breathing life into the maybe-dead. And no discussion of it, either.

They'd fallen, quickly and again to Sasha's surprise, into a companionable rhythm: caring for patients, cooking and eating together, tending the garden and the animals. Not only Puppy Dog, but the mule Jess kept for pulling the cart, as well as the stocky, oddly striped but unusually docile horse with the flat-top mane Sasha assumed she used for longer journeys. And they'd talked, as they worked and ate, and later, too, into the night - lying across the room from one another in their beds, about what felt to Sasha like everything and nothing, all at once.

She'd shared with Jess what little there was to share of her own life: her childhood back east and college days at Mount Holyoke; the broken engagement that had brought on a prolonged estrangement from her parents, and especially her mother; the years of travel that had begun to feel more like wandering, both before and after the accident that had stolen parts of her memory.

The apparition and its intermittent hauntings she omitted altogether.

Jess, she learned, was a mix of guarded and transparent, open and closed: sharing thoughts and feelings and impressions as freely as they came to her, or so it seemed to Sasha, but revealing almost nothing of her own background, her own history. She'd lived in the Spring a long time, years if not decades, but refused to be pinned down on *how* long, or even on how old she was - though Sasha was more certain than ever now that she couldn't be more than forty. She had no formal education to speak of, or so she claimed, but seemed to know a little of everything, from languages and mathematics to geology and botany and zoology - and to feel sufficiently confident in that knowledge to hold opinions, not just recite facts.

"The problem with Plato," she'd said one night, "is there's no room at all for subjectivity. You gonna tell me your idea of the perfect chair looks just the same as mine? Hell, mine might not even have legs."

Then, five minutes later: "You ever see one of those fish that walks around on its hands and feet? I think they might be my favorite kind of creature in the world. Pull off their arms or their tails, carve out their hearts, and they just grow 'em right on back. Unbelievable, really, the sort of thing the animal world comes up with, when it's left to its own devices. Plus they always kind of look like they're smiling, you know?"

She'd smiled too, right at Sasha, and something in Sasha's chest had risen and fallen and tightened - pleasurable and painful, hungering and full - and the smoke-wisp suspicions that had been growing in her since the day she'd come back to the house from the desert shaking and sick had solidified, there and then. Caused a part of her to panic, and another part of her, paradoxically, to fall still, to quieten and calm.

It wasn't new, the desire. Or maybe better to say it wasn't unfamiliar to her - although it had been years since she'd felt anything like it for another living being. There'd been limited options and even less inclination on her part while she'd been wandering, and the risks to her safety that the wrong approach to the wrong woman might have posed in some of the towns she'd passed through had seemed, at the time, to outweigh the need to satiate whatever fleeting impulse she might have felt. There'd been danger enough in her looking the way she did, in her wrapping the uncurved ranginess of her body in clothes intended for men; had been provocation enough, to some of the miners and cattle-hands and lawmen that she'd sat across from in so many bars, in her being a woman traveling alone at all.

Maybe it was only logical, she'd considered, that the proximity they'd been keeping would elicit something like it in her: that the warm practicality of Jess' manner, the soft fullness of her body, the genuine care she'd shown for Sasha after the dead boy in the desert would kindle ashes Sasha had left to burn out. Maybe she should've expected nothing else of herself, in the circumstances.

And she still remembered some of how she'd felt before - or thought she did. Some of the ways it had been with the girls at school and then at college, with another of the teachers at the academy she'd taught at back home - even if that last memory had been tarnished by the overlain veneer of her mother's disgust when she'd found the two of them together in Sasha's bedroom, the horrified widening of her mother's eyes and the names she'd shouted after Sasha as she'd thrown her and what few possessions Sasha had accumulated since Holyoke out onto the street.

Whether Jess felt anything like it for Sasha, of course - whether she was even aware that feelings like Sasha's were a possibility, that they were something that *were* and could *be* - was impossible to say. Although the breadth and manner of Jess' conversation suggested to Sasha that she might at the very least have heard of the *genre* of the thing before, the *category* of it - as an anthropological phenomenon, if not a lived experience.

"Y'alright in there?" Jess asked her, setting another lunch bowl down on the table by Sasha's clenching hand - not soup this time but vegetables, little parcels of rice and cabbage wrapped in some sort of vine leaf that she'd cooked up next to some fried eggplant and a smaller bowl of smashed garbanzo beans. "You look a hundred miles away."

"Sorry," Sasha said, shaking herself out of the reverie she'd been lost in, away from the tensed muscles of Jess' shoulders as she'd bent over the fire that had sent her thoughts skittering down a path they like as not shouldn't have. "Just, you know... went somewhere else for a second."

Jess bit her lip and shook her head in sympathy, and a hot pang of guilt like a momentary fever passed along Sasha's spine.

She thinks you mean the desert, she thought. *She thinks you were thinking about the boy out there. Maybe the other men too. She thinks it's got you traumatized, what you saw.*

"It'll fade, honey," Jess said, taking Sasha's hand and squeezing it gently – the physical contact combined with the unexpected endearment sending another, less scalding and altogether more welcome sensation down Sasha's back. "Not right away, but it'll fade."

Sasha nodded dumbly in return, afraid to speak.

"You just focus on what's in front of you for right now, okay? And maybe later you and me can go do a little planting and digging, take your mind off things. A little harvesting too, maybe. That black sage out there looks just about ready to pop."

She pointed to the window, to the herb garden beyond. Sasha followed the trajectory of the gesture, turning her eyes to the glass.

And almost fell out of her chair, when she saw what was out there.

The ghost – or apparition, or hallucination. The thing that stalked her: small and hunched and hooded, its off-white skin speckled with lesions.

Looking right at her - *staring* right at her, through the window.

Beckoning to her, with one clawed and rotting finger.

CHAPTER 6

The Assembly wasn't exactly a harvest festival, Jess said, and it wasn't exactly a thanksgiving, but was something closer to a prayer: a collective act of worship, inviting the land to give back to the congregants, to keep them fed - or fed enough - for another turn of the wheel.

The form of the thing was something like a party: a convocation of people from the Spring and the other settlements over, gathered together on the dirt path that was nominally the Spring's square to eat, drink and dance to whatever music the townsfolk felt inclined to muster, in the name of pleasing - or at the very least pacifying - whichever gods kept watch over the cattle, the crops and the town itself.

"It's tradition, mainly," Jess had added, almost apologetically. "Doubt many of them really believe it works. But they do it every year, just the same."

Though neither of them *had* to go, of course, she'd assured Sasha. Not if Sasha didn't feel up to it.

And as it happened: no, Sasha *didn't* feel up to it. She hadn't felt up to much of anything since she'd seen the apparition at the window, calling to her, although Jess couldn't have known that. All *Jess* knew was what she'd known before: that Sasha was still shaken up by the body in the desert.

Which worked for Sasha. What benefit could there be, after all, in letting slip that she was seeing things? Seeing *ghosts*, if that was even what they were?

Jess would be kind, and sympathetic, Sasha was sure - the way she'd be with any patient who came to her door with a delusion, with an obsessive thought or fantasy they couldn't shake. But a part of her would pity Sasha, too; would feel sorry that the contours of Sasha's apparently fragile mind had bent themselves into such odd and unsettling shapes. And if there was one thing Sasha didn't want, it was Jess' pity.

"I want to go," Sasha had replied, not so much because it was true as because she *wanted* it to be. Because even if the prospect of going to the damn thing filled her stomach with something like lead - the prospect of going *with Jess*, in Jess' company if not on her arm, was one she found she didn't want to turn down.

Jess had smiled then, and it had been enough for Sasha to forget - for as long as the smile lasted - near-on every reservation she'd had.

She'd need a change of clothes for the occasion, Jess told her: something clean and smart, even if it wasn't exactly formal. The townsfolk were sticklers for clean and smart, she said - at least where the Assembly was concerned. It wouldn't do for Sasha to look like she wasn't willing to scrub up, to put in a little effort.

The clothes on Sasha's back and the ones she'd carried with her through the desert *were* clean, in fact: it had been a point of pride for her to keep them that way, wherever the availability of running water would let her. They were very far from smart, though: their colors faded from the sun, the sand and dust just about baked into their creases, and more than a few holes and tears peppering their thinning fabrics. Jess, fortunately, had offered a solution: a tailor she knew from two towns over, who made house calls, and who'd refused to take Jess' money in exchange for his services ever since she'd helped his son recover from a riding accident that the doctor in his own town - a bad-tempered old coot with a fancy diploma he kept hanging on the wall of his office for everyone to see - had adamantly insisted would stop the kid from ever walking again.

"You'll be wanting a suit, not a dress, I'm guessing?" she'd asked Sasha, as casually as if she were enquiring whether Sasha wanted salt or chilli on her eggs. Sasha, dumbfounded, had mouthed a barely audible *sure* of acquiescence - and before the day was out, the tailor had arrived, to measure and fit her for her clothes to come.

He was a likeable man, jovial and quick to laugh and given to whistling to himself as he worked, and if *he* was surprised at being called upon to cut's a man's suit to a woman's body, then he was polite enough not to let on. The outfit he made came back just two days later, hand-delivered along with a bottle of cactus wine by the man's son: a soft grey jacket, pants and vest; a button-down shirt the color of a pine tree; cotton socks, and a brand-new pair of boots Sasha was surprised to find molded to the dimensions of her feet exactly, though the man hadn't measured them.

Jess' outfit had come hand-delivered too, by way of one of the sewing girls in the Spring: a length of silk going in at the waist and out at the hips, neither so ostentatious she could be accused of overdressing nor so simple that she'd ruffle any feathers by looking like she hadn't tried at all. Like as not, Sasha thought, she'd chosen it for practicality: for how quickly and straightforwardly she could move in it, if she needed to; how easily its sleeves could be ripped away to form a makeshift bandage or to tourniquet an unanticipated bleed.

They got themselves ready together, when the night came: Jess disappearing behind the cherry blossom-decorated dressing screen beside her bed, and Sasha exchanging her stained white shirt and bluejeans for those things the tailor had chosen for her, her back turned away from the screen, just in case. She did what she could not to stare, when Jess finally emerged again - the dress clinging to her body and her hair brushed down across the curve of her neck and the indented slope of her collarbone.

"You sure this is gonna be okay?" she asked - pointing down at herself, at the suit, hoping Jess would understand the question, the *will there be trouble if I show up like this?* she hadn't known exactly how to say. The follow up question she hadn't *wanted* to ask, namely:

If there will be trouble – is it gonna be a few scowls thrown at us over the punch bowl, or a couple closed fists thrown at my head when I step away from the herd?

Jess looked her up and down carefully; seemed to think hard before she responded.

"I'd tell you they ain't like that, in the Spring," she said, "and mostly they're not, in my experience. Men like the Sheriff and old Harlan up at the store... they don't give two shits what *anyone* does, *or* how they look, so long as it's not hurting anybody or bringing trouble down on the town. And Rooster... I've known that man a long time, and I know for a *fact* he couldn't care less about who's in shorts and who's in pantyhose."

"But if you were to ask me about a few of the others - Betsy Hacker at the drugstore, say, or that old bastard Ben who manages the bank – then, I don't know... maybe I'd have a worry. A little doubt, anyway, about how they'd take to a woman inclined to turn up to a party in what they'd think of as a man's suit. Even a woman who wears that suit as well as you wear *that* one."

Sasha felt a blush creep up her ears; tried to focus on keeping her breathing steady, her heartbeat slow.

"I'll tell you something, though," Jess continued, taking a lightweight shawl from the hat-rack by the door and draping it over the bare skin of her shoulders. "Neither Betsy nor Ben nor anyone like them is gonna dare say a damn thing about you, or *to* you, as long as you're there with me. Not unless they want to be setting their own bones when they fall down the cellar and break a wrist. Or treating it themselves, the next time they come down with a dose of the clap."

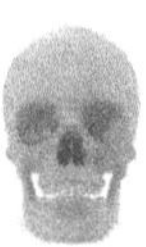

In the light of a hundred hanging lanterns, with the square separated off from the rest of the town by intersecting rows of picnic tables loaded with carved pumpkin heads and corn dolls, and with a band of drummers pounding out a rhythm on a makeshift stage of shipping crates, the Spring seemed almost beautiful: a far cry from the desolate patch of scorched earth nothing Sasha had encountered, the first time she and Puppy Dog had drifted through its limits.

There were a lot of people there, more than she'd seen in any one place in a very long time, and it took an effort of will to push back against the claustrophobia the experience brought on, the sensation of being penned in on all sides by the size and weight and smell of the crowd. And there *were* looks, despite Jess' reassurances. Not many, not enough for Sasha to feel unsafe or any more uncomfortable than she did already, but *some*: shocked, then disapproving eyes roaming from her suit to her face and back again, widening at the juxtaposition before narrowing in distaste at its unavoidable implication.

They bothered her less than she'd thought they might, though.

The formal aspects of the Assembly - what Jess had called *the ritualistic elements* - were over early on and quickly, seeming to amount to not much more than a few words of supplication from the Mayor and the setting alight of a half-dozen of the corn dolls on a raised central pyre no bigger than a campfire while the townsfolk looked on. The rest, the aftermath, really *was* a party: all dancing and drinking and laughter, with nothing to differentiate it, on the surface, from any other celebration Sasha had ever been to.

Rooster was there among the others, she noticed: not swinging his skeletal limbs around a partner or making animated conversation with an eligible widow, but watching from the side-lines, his thin fingers digging into a bottle of something dark and unidentifiable and his cadaverous features twisting into something like sardonic amusement as he took in the festivities around him. He saw Jess and Sasha, but didn't come over to say hi; only waved to them both from across the square, tipping two digits to his sunken temple in a salute that made no sense at all to Sasha, but which seemed to make Jess smile.

"You want to dance?" Jess asked her after a spell, gesturing to the swelling throng of bodies as the drummers on stage launched into another piece of music more insistent than the last, even if you couldn't quite call it a song.

No, she thought, trying and failing to remember the last time she'd danced, the last time she'd been anywhere where dancing had been on the cards - but nodded anyway, and let Jess lead her by the hand into the shifting crowd.

It was thoroughly chaste, as Sasha imagined dances went: one of Jess' hands resting lightly on her waist and another, with just as little pressure, on her shoulder. There were no stares thrown their way now, no quizzical looks from bank clerks and drugstore gossips; only movement and heat and the unanticipated relief of a body - Jess' body - close to hers, inviting her to relax, to forget the rest.

Then, from nowhere: the pull and clatter of a lever, not outside but *in* her, and the smell of cypress trees and firedamp flooding her bloodstream.

And an image, arriving in her head in present tense with sudden and absolute clarity. A picture, or a memory.

Not one apparition but a dozen, more: twenty, thirty, a platoon of them, as white-skinned and black-eyed as the thing that's been haunting her, stalking her. The hoods she might have expected are absent here, and the small, hunched frames of the creatures are swaddled in something like sackcloth - their heads and necks exposed, entirely visible.

They're bald, every one of them, their scalps smooth and free of even the lightest down. They'd almost be polished-looking, but for the green-gray lesions that pit them like mold spores, like mildew on a washcloth.

And they're singing, chanting: their wide mouths - unnaturally wide, far wider than any human's, and lined with supernumerary rows of tiny, pointed teeth - seeming to dislocate as easily as a snake's with the release of every elongated syllable.

The dozen of them - the twenty or thirty or more of them - are standing over something. Looking down at it: jostling for position, vying with one another for a better view. Something laid out not quite on the ground but nevertheless below them - spread out like a sacrifice on a low stone table.

It's a man, down there. Or, really, a boy: shirtless and sweating, fit and strong, but scarcely - in her estimation - even a day older than seventeen.

For the moment at least, he's alive.

Alive, but in agony: his body writhing and bucking and arching on the table, fighting against the shackles that hold him there. He's screaming, or he seems to be, but no sound at all emerges from his throat that she can hear. His vocal cords are gone, she thinks. He's been screaming so loudly and for so long, he's torn the elastic tissues there to shreds.

Of why he's screaming, why he's in such excruciating pain, she has no sense at all. The chanting things - they're looking at him but not touching him, laying not a single hand on his flailing body.

Whatever's hurting him - it's coming from the inside, *not the outside.*

She's been watching him, she realizes, from among the horde of lesioned things - as one of them. And now he's turning his head to look right at her, training his wild eyes directly on hers. Silver eyes, bright as bullets.

Kill me, he says. Please, God - just kill me.

Sasha blinked, the closing and opening of her own eyelids so slow as to be snakelike, and the picture and all its instantaneity faded - dissolving back into nothing as Jess and the Assembly and the townsfolk burst back into living color, crowding out the afterimage of the boy and the table and the apparitions.

"Sasha?" she heard Jess say, her voice shot through with worry. "Sasha, can you talk to me?"

"I don't...," she started to answer. And then she was falling, the ground collapsing under her, and there was nothing to see but green and gray and silver.

CHAPTER 7

Getting home from the Spring was a kind of blur, although Sasha had an idea that Rooster had helped Jess to carry her out of the square and into a buggy, somewhere along the line.

She started to come back to herself more or less as soon as the door was closed and Jess had set a fire for the kettle - the transition to full alertness, full awareness of her surroundings from the dim half-consciousness that had overtaken her at the Assembly something a little like waking from sleep into an unfamiliar bed, in an unlit room, and very nearly as jarring.

"Better?" Jess said, her back still turned away from the easy chair she - or maybe Rooster - had settled Sasha into.

"Yes, thank you," Sasha answered, wondering how in the hell Jess had known when to ask, how she'd got a bead on the *exact* moment Sasha had come to fully occupy her body again.

"Glad to hear it. Now, here - I made you something. So you just drink it, okay? It'll make you feel that much better again, I guarantee it."

She spun around on her heels; had crossed the room and pressed a warm cup of something that smelled like rosemary and sage and sea salt into Sasha's hands more quickly than Sasha would have thought possible, if she'd stopped to think about it at all.

"It's lavender," she added, before Sasha could ask. "From out front."

Sasha smiled at her weakly over the rim of the cup and took a sip - relieved to find, when the tea hit her tastebuds, that it went down easily. By the fourth sip, she'd even come to enjoy it a little.

"I'm sorry," she began, conscious of the early stirrings of what she thought would eventually blossom into acute embarrassment. "I didn't mean to ruin your night like that. Or to call so much attention to myself, come to that."

Jess waved away the apology; picked up a stool from over by the fireplace and brought it near to the armchair, close enough to Sasha to be comforting but not so close as to make her feel crowded, claustrophobic.

"It happen a lot?" she said, sitting down. "You fainting, losing time?"

"Not often. Occasionally."

"You ever talk to anyone about it?"

Sasha shook her head. When had she last talked to anyone at all, about *anything*, for long enough to warrant bringing *this* up? Anyone but Jess, anyway?

"It's not for me to say it'd help any," Jess continued. "Talking... it can be good sometimes, sure. Cathartic, if there are things inside a person that they're bottling up but want to let out, if only someone else'd ask the right question. Other times, though... maybe not. Other times, talking's no better than picking at a scab. Just prodding it and poking it and jabbing it with a thumbnail so it never stops bleeding. And you probably know better than I do which one of them is true for you."

And other times *again*, Sasha thought, it isn't a choice between talking and not talking. Because how are you supposed to talk about something you can't explain in words, that makes no kind of sense even to you? Something that can't *be* told, because it has no shape, no beginning or middle or end, that isn't really anything at all but sounds and smells and pictures?

"I don't know that there's very much to talk about," she said quietly. "But thank you, I guess. If that was you offering to listen to me."

Jess reached for her across the space between them, laying one open palm across Sasha's clenched fist; she smiled, eyes soft, and it felt to Sasha a lot like breaking the surface after too long struggling to breathe underwater.

Whether she kissed Sasha, or whether Sasha kissed her, Sasha couldn't have said afterward. But whichever of them started it, the other seemed more than happy to go on, to pick up the thread of the other. It was slow and gentle, until it wasn't - and then Sasha's shirt was untucked and unbuttoned, and Jess' dress was unfastened and halfway down her back.

Sasha's hand went to Jess' breast. Jess sighed at the touch and slid her palms down to rest on Sasha's collarbone - before pushing her, lightly but firmly, away.

"You sure you want this?" she said, with an uncertainty Sasha had never heard from her before. "You weren't looking so great before, what with the passing out and all, and I kinda feel like maybe I'm breaching some sort of duty of care here. Like maybe I'm taking advantage of you a little."

And at that, Sasha could really only smile back.

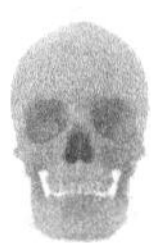

Jess hadn't mentioned the scars, during: had been quick enough to run her fingers over them, and then her tongue, but hadn't called attention to them, hadn't asked Sasha what they meant or how she'd got them. Which, Sasha reflected as she lay back against the pillows - Jess resting in the groove between her neck and shoulder as she caught her breath - showed either tremendous restraint or an unexpected lack of curiosity.

Because the scars - they were far and away the central feature of Sasha's body, neck to toe.

She made a point of not looking too closely at them, even when she washed herself: at turning her face away from the faded pink and silver lines crisscrossing her chest, her back, her legs, the length of both arms almost to the wrist. But she couldn't help but be cognizant of them on her skin. On the parts of it she could see, and the parts of it she couldn't - even if she didn't understand herself how they'd come to be there.

"You can ask," she said, taking the bull by the horns.

"About what?"

"These."

She gestured down at one of the scars on her stomach: a narrow, raised stripe of thickened tissue cutting from her hip to just above her pubic bone.

Jess watched her trace its trajectory in the air above the flesh; took in the scar itself, her eyebrows wrinkling in what Sasha read as genuine interest rather than disgust.

She's a doctor, Sasha reminded herself. *Or the closest thing to it around here. She probably knows better than to let herself react to any of the strangenesses a body can fall prey to.*

"You *want* me to ask?" Jess replied eventually, sounding relaxed and sated still, in spite of the turn the conversation had taken.

"You don't want to know where I got them?"

"Well... sure, I guess." She traced a fingertip over another of the scars - a shorter, more ragged mark spanning the front half of one of Sasha's upper ribs. "If that's something you wanna tell me."

She *did* want to tell her, Sasha realized. She only wished she had something more to tell.

"I think it is," she said. "Except... I don't exactly know."

If she'd been anticipating surprise, outright shock even, she'd have been disappointed.

"You don't know where?" Jess said evenly. "Okay. You know *when*? You remember when they first showed up on you like that?"

It wasn't something Sasha had been asked before, by anyone. But to *that*, if not to the rest of the conundrum, she had an answer.

"You know I told you I had an accident?" she started. "Or maybe... not an accident, I don't know. And that I came around up north, but couldn't work out how I got there?"

Jess nodded against the crook of her neck, apparently listening intently.

"So, these... *these* are one of the things I woke up with. They were kinda... left over from whatever it was that happened to me before I got there."

She'd been horrified to find them, when she'd finally stumbled out of the ice and the wind into the fetid warmth of a cowshed and stripped off the furs she had no memory of ever having owned. Horrified, and bewildered: not only by the presence of the scars, but by their condition.

They hadn't been fresh.

She'd been certain they should have been bleeding - or if not bleeding then clotting, coagulating, mending at the edges. The bones and muscles underneath had felt that way: as if they were still healing, still trying to find a way to repair themselves. But while the skin had looked sore and red, looked damaged - so very, very damaged... it hadn't looked *recently* damaged. It was more, she'd thought at the time, like whatever had happened to it had happened weeks before. Maybe even *months* before.

"And you think you got 'em here," Jess said - not as a question, but as a statement, a call-back to what Sasha had told her early on about her reasons for coming to the Spring, for coming *back* to the Spring. "Out in the desert. In the mines."

"Maybe." Sasha shrugged - not so hard as to dislodge Jess from her shoulder, but enough to signal her hesitancy. "Maybe not. Guess I'll find out soon."

Jess was quiet for a moment; was contemplating something, or so Sasha thought.

"What *do* you remember?" she said eventually. "Not about what happened to you, I know that part is kind of... lost. But about... before, I guess. *Before* it happened."

Sasha thought hard before she answered - struggling to marshal what fragments of recollection had been left her into something like coherence.

"Right before? It's sort of... hazy." But no, not hazy, that wasn't right. *Foggy.* Foggy, that was what she meant: words and actions and events that should have been immediately accessible, should have been *right there* in the cabinet of her mind now steeped in fog as thick as syrup. *Buried* in it, with not so much as the outline of them visible from a distance of time. "There was an argument, maybe. Some kind of... disagreement. Shouting."

"Who with?"

A woman, Sasha thought. Two women, maybe: one older, one younger, the younger one more familiar to her than the other. Similar voices, mellow and drawling and West-accented. Anger, pulsing like a toxin through the both of them.

"I don't know," she said, and it was an honest reply, in a way, because she couldn't have told Jess the names of either with a gun against her head. But it was a dishonest one, too - because she was pretty sure they were important, these women. That they'd meant something to her, once.

Meant more than just *something*, maybe.

CHAPTER 8

She couldn't put off going back to the mines forever, and she knew it. Jess knew it too, she thought. Or, at least, didn't try to dissuade her - not when she woke up one morning, Jess' still half-sleeping body pressed tight against hers the way it had been every morning for the last few weeks before, and made the decision to go, and go *then*, that same day. Just wrapped a clean red rag around Sasha's neck to keep the dust from her face; pushed a fresh canteen of water into Sasha's hands, and dropped a small, sad kiss to Sasha's cheek as she walked outside to collect the Mustang from the stable.

The ride out to the desert was as hot and gritty and uncomfortable as it had been before, made more so as the journey wore on and Puppy Dog's apprehension at returning to the scene of the earlier crime grew impossible to ignore - the nervous, jerking motions of his legs and flank and hips tossing her this way and that in the saddle.

A part of her had anticipated finding another dead boy by the open mine entrance; had been preparing for it almost since Jess had watched her leave from the doorway of the house Sasha was beginning to think of as *their house*. But there was none that she could see: no body, nor any taste or smell of putrefaction that might suggest one on the dry air.

No sound, either; no sound at all. All around her, the desert was quiet - as still and lifeless as a catacomb.

She'd packed a tool this time, a hook-ended fire iron that had slid easily into Puppy Dog's saddlebag, and she reached for it as she clambered down from his back, clamping it between her fists in an overhand grip that left her knuckles three shades lighter than the rest of her skin. In the absence of a stake or any other kind of post, she left him untied; let him graze - if any kind of grazing was possible - on the sand. Could only hope he'd choose to stay close, and not wander too far from wherever she ended up being.

With the fire iron in her hand, the piled planks and fallen boulders came away easily from the mouth of the mine, carving out a walkway broad and tall enough for her to slip through - far bigger than the crawlspace she'd initially worried she'd have to traverse on her knees.

And so, back straight and chin high, the fire iron twirling from one set of fingers like a Bowie knife and the safety lamp that Jess had given her hanging from the other, she stepped inside.

It was dark, of course; exactly as dark as she'd expected, the reddish desert light dwindling to a shaft and then a pinprick as she edged further in, further down. When even the pinprick began to recede and there was nothing to see in the darkness but the dim green luminescence of what she took to be a fungus or an algae climbing the walls around and above her like vines, she set the lamp to burn, praying - just as she'd prayed for Puppy Dog to stay - that the lighting of it wouldn't catch a fire in whatever underground gases might have her surrounded.

Illuminated, the mine was more mundane and less threatening than she'd feared: a narrow tunnel burrowing through a wall of dark brown rock, the rock salted with purplish crystals and threaded, just as she'd thought, with what might have been mushrooms or moss. No rail tracks on the ground, but the sloping dirt path under her leading down at an angle not quite so steep that she'd lose her footing if she followed it.

She walked.

She'd been walking long enough to build a thirst that made her suck down the water in the canteen like a baby at a bottle when she heard the first set of footsteps, close by or up ahead – and deep enough in the belly of the mountain by then to have trouble knowing from the echo of them alone just how near or not they were to her. They were fast, though; scuttling, spider-like. Multiple.

Three or four sets of them, she guessed. Three or four bodies, moving quickly in the dark.

She stopped, for just a second; weighed up turning around, turning back.

A second later, they were on her.

There were five of them, not four: the smallest so short and so thin that its feet might have left no sound-impression at all on the dirt. Five mottled, fish-belly white heads on slight, hunched bodies hung with brown sackcloth robes, mouths too big and ink-black eyes too small.

Apparitions.

Except... no. That wasn't quite right. Wasn't quite *all*.

The creatures she'd seen before, in Boone and Cooper Bridge, by the dead boy in the desert and calling to her through the thick glass of Jess' window... they'd seemed not entirely material, not entirely *there*. They hadn't walked through walls, hadn't rattled their chains or dissolved into transparency, but there was something insubstantial about them anyway; something that made it easy for her to think of them as ghosts, as spectres. As shadows of the real, not as real in themselves.

These things, though - they were solid, unmistakably corporeal. She could smell them, the methane and mildew stench of them catching in her craw as they formed a circle around her, penning her in. Could feel them, the bones of the wasted fingers that were really more like claws cutting into her at the wrists and shoulders and scraping at the scars across her chest and stomach as they pushed and pulled her. Could hear them, the hissing of their breath and the gnashing of their piranha teeth as they snarled at her.

She fought them off, or tried to - whirled at them with her elbows and her knees, slashing at them with the fire iron and aiming kicks with the balls of her feet at their hairless heads and concave stomachs. But they were too fast and too many, snatching the lamp and the iron from out of her hands and throwing them both to the ground. The lamp rolled, casting strange shadows across the glowing walls; flickered, briefly, then died, taking what light it gave with it and throwing the mine into absolute darkness.

What came next was nothing but sensation: her hair pulled backward, exposing her throat; the grooves of a paw-like palm across her mouth, swallowing her screams; too-long arms around her waist, holding her still.

Rough fibres under her nostrils - a cloth or a pad. Nauseating sweetness in her airways.

A deeper blackness, absolute and suffocating.

CHAPTER 9

A doctor's office: that was her first thought, when her eyes came open and she was able to look around. A compact doctor's office, carved out of a mountain and lit with oil lamps glowing blue not orange - and plastered to the stone wall, an anatomical outline of a pencil-sketched skeleton that was both too short in the legs and too wide in the skull to be entirely human.

There were tools laid out on a trolley in one corner of what she had to think of as the room: pliers and scalpels, sharp-bladed scissors and dull-edged saws. Surgical instruments, much like the ones Jess kept in the house for her patients, but in altogether worse condition - dull where Jess' were polished, rusty and corroded where Jess' were neatly kept and clean. In the opposite corner were medicines, or the brown-tinted bottles that suggested them, arranged in ascending size order on a cabinet fashioned from a marbled wood the color of blood that was like no wood Sasha had ever seen before.

She was lying down, she realized - body stretched out on a rectangular table that felt cold and hard under the base of her spine and the palms of her hands. It was metal, she guessed; metal or granite, something dense and unyielding.

She wasn't strapped down, at least - not like a prisoner, not like the boy she'd dreamed up or remembered the night of the Assembly. But whatever the creatures that had ambushed her had used to knock her out, whatever concoction they'd soaked into the cloth they'd pressed to her nose and mouth in the seconds before she'd slipped into what must have been unconsciousness, it had left her depleted: so weak she found herself struggling to lift her arms, and with an idea, even before she tried and failed to do it, that getting up from the table would be almost impossible.

"You're awake," said a voice from somewhere above and behind her, somewhere unseeable from her current position. "Good. How are you feeling?"

It wasn't a voice she recognized. And it was... off-kilter, somehow: the harmonics and the timber of it *wrong*, in a way she couldn't entirely place, and the accent alien to her, though it spoke in faultless English. There were traces of what might on the surface have been French in there, and what might have been Russian, but was nothing like either, not in any meaningful sense. Her first impression, upon hearing it, was that it wasn't really human - although she was quick to dismiss the notion, as much because of the fear it drove into her as because it seemed unlikely, impossible.

When she didn't respond immediately, the throat the voice belonged to - the throat it *had* to belong to, since she'd picked up on no other presence in the room with her - coughed: a wet, spongy, tuberculous sound that made her think of damp rooms and incipient infection. Then the *body* it belonged to seemed to move - its feet tapping out the same scuttling arachnid arpeggio on the stone floor below as the things that had come after her. That had succeeded in bringing her here, wherever *here* was.

It's one of them, she thought, the suspicion crystallizing into knowledge as it glid around the edges of the table, stopping only when it reached the bottom - where, if she craned her neck, they were near-on facing one another.

It was white, like the others; its bald head and face speckled with the same green spore-like lesions and its eyes black holes carved out of the sockets. It wore the same brown robes - although *its* robe, she noticed, was draped with a purple sash embroidered with a complex silver insignia. A wave, maybe; a current passing over water.

The effect, when it spoke again, was jarring: intelligible language, *polite* language - or so it struck her - having no right to fall from that sharp-toothed mouth, that dislocating serpent's jaw.

"I expect the drops will wear off shortly," it said, matter-of-factly - studying her where she lay with a kind of expectant curiosity. "I don't know how much they used, I'm afraid. I *told* them not to use *anything*, but they're not great thinkers, the guardsmen, and I'm sure you remember how heavy-handed they can be, when they believe they're under threat."

Remember? she thought. *He thinks I* remember *being here? That I know those things, those... guardsmen, or whatever they are?*

Have *I been here?* Should *I remember?*

"Why did they bring me down here?" she asked. "Why did you send them? What do you *want* with me?"

The thing's forehead creased, lesions collapsing into the skin folds the sudden change in expression created. If it were a person, she might've said it looked puzzled.

"*Bring* you?" It cocked its mottled head to one robed shoulder, definitely confused now. "I mean... yes, I asked them to... *collect* you from the Mesial, though I stress again that I specifically asked them not to be... forceful in their approach. But *you* came to *us*, Sasha. You brought *yourself* home."

She felt the impact of the word as keenly as if the thing had struck her with them, and not just uttered them aloud: in the churning of her stomach, the tingling in her scalp, the ringing in her ears.

Home.

The thing, the creature - it thought she'd *come home.* That she belonged there, with it and the other things like it in the dark underground.

And maybe you do, another voice whispered to her - one that sounded, to her rising horror, very like her own. *You're the one that's been wanting to come back here, for so long you can't even recollect how long it's been.*

Maybe there's a reason for that. And maybe it's not just about those scars across your chest.

"What are you talking about?" she said, near to gulping down her own tongue as she choked out the question. "How is this *home*?"

The creature's frown unravelled, a kind of awareness rippling across its features.

"You don't remember," it said, flat and hollow. Then, after a beat: "what *do* you remember?"

It was the same thing Jess had asked her, that first night in bed; the same question she'd asked herself, over and over again, in all the time she'd been wandering, drifting from town to town and place to place with some part of her always half-focused on unlocking the chest that held whatever memories she'd lost inside of it.

"I don't know," she replied, too exhausted and addled and at war with herself to try to stitch what scattered images she had into a whole, to even try to hide her confusion from the monster standing over her. "My mother. My family. Some other people, maybe." She paused. "I think maybe it's been a long time since I've seen them."

Silence hung between them for a moment. The creature's black eyes blinked, then seemed - improbably - to soften in sympathetic understanding, the muscles around them relaxing as it took her in.

"Amnesia," it said eventually, as if delivering a diagnosis. "Some confabulation too, perhaps. The two do tend to go together, don't they? To complement one another. Where there's a gap that lacks an explanation, the mind will seek to plug it, however it can, and no matter the veracity. It's a tendency, a very natural tendency. I can't tell exactly why it's happened here, but I'd say that trauma would have been involved somewhere. The trauma of... leaving here, perhaps. Of being thrust back... out there, even of your own volition."

Abruptly, it shifted a quarter-turn away from her, and took off for the medicine cabinet with the same scuttling motion it had used to reach her - leaving her, still helpless, on the table, what few memories she'd *thought* she could rely on dashed to splinters on the rocks.

A heartbeat later, and the creature was back where it had been, a cup no bigger than a thimble gripped between two elongated fingers.

"Are you able to sit up?" it asked her.

She shook her head, and, reading her response, it inched up the table and toward her; lowered the tiny cup to her closed mouth.

"Lethe water," it said quietly - seeing her stiffen, seeing her bite down on her lips to keep them together. "For forgetting, in so many cases. But occasionally for remembering, too, where remembered things are lost already. Drink, please. It will... do you some good."

Again, she shook her head, this time with sufficient violence that the creature took a step away from the table; clasped a second, protective hand over the cup to stop its liquid contents spilling.

"Please," it repeated. "If you want to remember... please."

She ought to resist, she knew: ought to fight and keep fighting, do anything she could to stop the creature poisoning her - poisoning her *again* - with whatever toxin it seemed intent on forcing into her.

But she was tired - so damn tired. Tired of fighting, tired of hiding, tired of wandering. Tired of not knowing who she was now, or where she'd been, or whatever the hell had happened to her to make her what she'd become.

So. Damn. Tired.

And so, when the creature bent cautiously back over her with its thimbleful of medicine and pressed the cup to her lips, she *stopped* fighting. Let it pour the liquid into her mouth; swallowed as the acid-burn sweetness of it hit her tastebuds.

Let go. Let herself remember.

CHAPTER 10
Before

They were fighting even before they passed Redondo Beach, sniping passive-aggressively at one another over everything from the volume of the radio to Sasha's posture in the passenger seat: the way she pressed her knees against the glove box and her cheek against the headrest, slipping off her glasses as if she was getting ready to take a nap.

"You're just gonna, what? Fall asleep and let me drive you?" Ingrid said, irritation threatening to slide all the way into full-blown anger.

"I thought maybe you wanted me to shut up," Sasha told her, hating how she sounded, the whining thread of martyrdom in the reply. Hating how quickly she'd let herself rise to the bait.

It wasn't entirely Ingrid's fault, the dark cloud that had settled over them since they'd hit the I-15. Ingrid was anxious, Sasha knew it, and anxiety had a habit of making her bad-tempered, making her lash out at whoever happened to be closest to her - which, here and now, was Sasha. It didn't mean anything, or anything much; wasn't the damning indictment of her feelings for Sasha or the state of their relationship it might have seemed to someone not familiar with the context, with the reason for the little road-trip they were taking.

Sasha, for her part, still couldn't have said for sure why she'd agreed to the trip in the first place. Meeting other people's parents had never been high up on her agenda, and she'd been with Ingrid less than six months – and only *dating* her, at that, not living in her apartment in Torrance or planning their wedding or speculating with her over the names of their future children. It hadn't once occurred to Sasha, before Ingrid had brought it up, that they were anywhere close to the point in the relationship where hopping into Ingrid's Jeep and powering down to her family's ranch in the back-end of the fucking desert would strike either one of them as a good idea.

But here they were, anyway.

She had an inkling, unconfirmed though it was, that Ingrid bringing her along to the ranch for the weekend - more or less *insisting* that she came along, even when the invitation made Sasha a little awkward, a little uncomfortable - had as much to do with Ingrid wanting to prove something to her folks as it had to do with Sasha herself, or with any desire Ingrid might have had to show her off or make a public commitment to the two of them building a life together.

That Ingrid wanted to hammer home a point, and Sasha was a prop to help her do it.

This is who I am. This is how I live. Take it or leave it.

She should've said no, she thought; should've made a stronger case for why she didn't want to be there, why Ingrid really ought to go alone, if she went at all. But she *hadn't* said no; she'd given in and chosen what had seemed the path of least resistance over an argument that would keep her up all night and tire her out for work the next day. And this, right now, was the upshot, the inevitable outcome of that in-the-moment pusillanimity: two days in the hinterland with a pair of socially conservative cattle-ranchers primed to hate her guts for no other reason than the fact of her existence, and a girlfriend who, it was dawning on her, she wasn't even sure she wanted to be seeing in another six months.

Great job, Diaz, you fucking coward. Great fucking job.

"Guess it must be weird for you, heading away from the city," Ingrid said - conversational, ostensibly, but with a bite to the not-quite-question that set Sasha's teeth on edge. "I know you get nervous when you stray too far from a Wi-Fi connection and a caramel macchiato."

Sasha took a breath; pressed her nails to her palms to keep her temper in check.

"I'm from New England," she answered, just about as neutrally as she could. "It's not like today's my first time stepping out into the middle of nowhere."

Ingrid bristled, visibly, at the wheel, and Sasha could have kicked herself for having replied at all.

It was never like this with Aurelia, she thought - then felt immediately guilty for having allowed herself to think it, as if the comparison itself represented a kind of infidelity.

Though the fact remained, it never *was*, with Aurelia; never *had* been.

It had been easy, with her: that was Sasha's abiding memory of the way things had been between them. Easy, and kind - *their* relationship characterized by the sort of reciprocal tenderness that she knew was largely absent between her and Ingrid. Sasha had never needed to have her guard up, with Aurelia; never needed to worry that she'd say the wrong thing, drop in the wrong cadence or the wrong intonation at the wrong moment and send everything spiraling into hot, angry chaos with a Rube Goldberg velocity.

The breakup had been gentle, too: a case of wrong place, wrong time above any fundamental incompatibility between them. Even her mother's reaction on stumbling on the two of them in bed together in Sasha's old studio in Santa Monica - surprise, then revulsion, then very vocal condemnation that continued even after Sasha noted, she thought entirely reasonably, that it was *her* studio to do whatever she liked in, with whomever she liked, and that her mother might have avoided seeing what she'd seen had she actually picked up the phone and alerted Sasha to her imminent arrival instead of just letting herself in with the spare key under the mat... it had been barely a bump in the otherwise smoothly-unfolding trajectory of the almost-year that she and Aurelia were together.

If it hadn't been for the very particular circumstances in which they'd met, Sasha halfway believed they wouldn't have broken up at all: that they'd be living *together* in the studio, fielding the occasional disgruntled call from Sasha's mother back in Boston and assembling flat-pack furniture on the weekends. But the circumstances were something more than infelicitous – they'd conspired against them from the start. Though Aurelia hadn't then turned forty, and Sasha was coming up on thirty herself, and though the power differential between them would in any other situation have been negligible, the facts were stark and unavoidable. Sasha had been a grad student in Aurelia's department, with Aurelia as her advisor, no less; Aurelia had been up for tenure at the small women's college that had brought them together; the college itself took a dimmer view than most on student-teacher romance, and an almost-year of surreptitious dates and not holding hands in the street and having to look back over their shoulders for over-interested faculty members whenever they were out in public had taken a significant toll on the health and happiness of both of them, by the end.

Sasha had been the one to call it off, eventually, one tearful, painfully-protracted Sunday morning after a night at the movies, where they'd bumped into one of Aurelia's older, fustier colleagues and his equally starch-collared wife, and where Aurelia had been forced into an on-the-spot lie about why she and Sasha should have found themselves at the theater together on what looked very much like the date it was - a lie so obvious and poorly-constructed that Sasha was embarrassed on her behalf. The colleague had been polite enough, before he and his wife had extricated themselves from the conversation to the relief of all concerned - but Aurelia had been so flustered, so shaken by the encounter that they'd ended up skipping the movie altogether and going back to her apartment, where she'd cried solidly for at least two hours before collapsing into spent, defeated sleep in the crook of Sasha's arm.

On some level, perhaps even a conscious one, Sasha had assumed that the breakup would be temporary, a quick fix for a short-term problem - and that, at some unspecified point after she'd finished up her thesis and graduated, they'd find each other again and pick up where they'd left off. It was something more than a surprise, then, when Aurelia left not just the university but the *city*, to take up a tenured post at a state college in the Midwest - and that Sasha found out not from Aurelia herself, who'd stopped returning her calls, but from a departmental email informing the students *en masse* that she'd gone and urging them to wish her all the very best in her new position.

Sasha had been heartbroken. And maybe it was inevitable, therefore, that any subsequent relationship in which found herself would be judged against what she'd had with Aurelia - however unfair that might have been. And Ingrid wasn't *bad*, after all; wasn't *wrong* for Sasha, in any way that Sasha could easily quantify. She just wasn't entirely *right*, either.

They drove mostly in silence for much of the rest of the morning, Ingrid's jaw clenching tighter and tighter as they moved inland and closer to the Nevada border.

"You sure you want to do this?" Sasha said after a while, moving a hand to Ingrid's leg in what she hoped would be read as a gesture of reconciliation, a desire for détente. "You sure it's gonna be okay?"

"Of course I'm sure," Ingrid snapped back at her, shaking off the hand with a twitch and a tensing of her thigh muscles. "Jesus, you think I'd have asked you to come if I wasn't? *Yes*, it's gonna be okay."

It wasn't, though.

They got to the ranch around lunchtime, greeted outside the house by the parents: a thin-faced, heavily made-up sixty-something white woman in a yellow pantsuit and her sunburned, denim-draped husband, his own face like a helium balloon wrapped in corrugated skin.

Their initial warmth toward their daughter and wary civility toward Sasha gave way to outright hostility in just about the time it took for the mother to pour them coffee, for the father to load a cup with cream and sugar and down it in three gulps and for Ingrid to introduce Sasha as her girlfriend. Things went downhill immediately thereafter: the mother spitting her disappointment, the father thunderously silent, Ingrid screaming back at them that this was *her life* and *her choice* and Sasha staring down at her feet on the deerskin rug, wishing she was anywhere else in the world but there.

To her immense relief, they left the ranch soon afterward, Ingrid more or less dragging Sasha to the Jeep by her elbow, as if Sasha had any intention of resisting - as if any part of her would have *wanted* to stay.

"Are you okay?" Sasha asked her, very tentatively, as they accelerated into the winding, arid length of empty desert road separating the ranch from the nearest unincorporated settlement - what had looked to Sasha's metropolitan eyes like some sort of mining town out of a Western.

"No," Ingrid told her - not looking at her but staring straight ahead at the horizon, like Sasha wasn't there at all. "No, I'm not fucking *okay*. Would *you* be okay, after that? God."

"I'm sorry. I was just asking."

"Well *stop* asking. It's not helpful."

Another silence, stretching out between them with the tensile strength of a rubber band.

"They'll come around," Sasha said, when the air in the car had grown so suffocating that she thought one of them might choke on it. "Give it time, and they'll come around."

"What, like *your* Mom did?" Ingrid squeezed a fist around the wheel; narrowed her eyes.

"She's... not a representative sample, you know that. She's got issues."

Religion, was what she meant; *she's got religion*. It was her lifelong, bone-deep devotion to the church - to the old bigot in the dog-collar at St.

Augustine and the even older bigot just installed in the Vatican - that was, at least as Sasha saw it, the real stumbling block to Marisol Diaz' acceptance of her daughter's sexuality; of *that lifestyle,* as she'd framed it, whenever she'd been left with no choice to put a name to it at all.

Ingrid's parents were churchgoers too, she knew; Lutherans, she thought, although quite what that meant in practical terms was as much a mystery to a dyed-in-the-wool atheist like Sasha as the mind-body problem or the functional necessity of dreaming. But the odds were good, or so she reasoned, that they weren't *quite* so wedded to God and the Baby Jesus as her own mother; that there was a solid chance they could be swayed by reason, by logic, by appeals to a basic humanity above and beyond whatever interpretation of the scriptures they were accustomed to.

"This was a mistake," Ingrid said, through gritted teeth. "You shouldn't have come."

"You *told* me to come."

"Yeah, well - I shouldn't have done. We should've both known better."

The unfairness of the statement - of the accusation implicit in it - hit Sasha like a blow to the chest.

"It's not like I even *wanted* to do this," she replied, before she had the sense to stop herself. "This was *your* idea, not mine."

"What the fuck is *that* supposed to mean? You were just, what? Humoring me? Playing along?"

There was corrosive edge lacing the mounting fury in Ingrid's voice now, a bitter incandescence that Sasha wasn't certain she'd ever heard from her before - and she found herself, if not frightened, then more than a little apprehensive of what Ingrid might say to her next, of what she might do.

"No," she started, trying to placate her, to pour water and not oil on the fire, "no, that wasn't what..."

A jolt and a jerk, and she was pitched forward in her seat - so far forward that her head almost connected with the windshield. It took her a second to work out that Ingrid had slammed on the brakes; that she'd stopped the Jeep dead in the center of the road.

"Get out," Ingrid snarled, still refusing to so much as turn her body Sasha's way.

Sasha glanced left and then right out of the Jeep's windows; saw nothing but dry hills and desert and the occasional sprouting cactus on either side.

"You're kidding, right?" She sat herself back upright; took in a lungful of air to steady her breathing. "It's a fucking wasteland out there. What am I supposed to do, *walk* back to L.A.?"

When Ingrid answered, it was in the same low, faintly dangerous growl she'd used before.

"It's half a mile to Ellacott from here. It's not big, but there'll be cell signal, and somewhere there to pick up a rental. You can drive yourself back to the city."

"Ingrid..."

"Get *out*, Sasha. Now. I can't even stand to look at you, let alone be sitting next to you the rest of the day."

She *wasn't* joking, Sasha knew; wasn't playing, or trying to scare Sasha into an apology. She was serious. And, crazy though it seemed, she most likely wouldn't budge a millimeter until Sasha did what she said and got her ass out of the Jeep and onto the side of what passed for a road in this godforsaken end of the universe.

Might even get proactive about it and try to *throw* Sasha out, or worse.

Ingrid wasn't a tall woman, or particularly strong; Sasha had four inches and maybe twenty pounds on her, most of the latter muscle. But she had a temper, a vicious one: Sasha had witnessed it in action more than a handful of times in the months she'd known her, when a waitress had messed up her dinner order or she'd broken the heel of a shoe or her cab driver had taken her a different route home than the one she'd demanded. It was one of the things that had first made Sasha question whether they really were compatible; that had made her wonder whether dating Ingrid was something she wanted to be doing at all, come Thanksgiving.

That temper - it wasn't something that could be reasoned with.

Sasha *did* have her cell, at least - and though she couldn't fathom why, it had signal, even out here. She had water, too: the almost-full bottle of it she'd bought with her for the journey but had been too wound up to drink. So, while it wouldn't be ideal to be trudging through half a mile of desert heat on a summer afternoon, assuming Ingrid was telling her the truth about the distance to the nearest town... it probably wouldn't kill her.

And, pathetic though she knew it was: letting Ingrid kick her out and leave her stranded in the wilderness at least took the decision to break up - to make a *clean* break - well and truly out of Sasha's hands.

'Alright,' she conceded. "Alright. I'm going."

Ingrid didn't respond; didn't even *look* at her.

Sasha sighed - partly out of frustration at the ludicrousness of Ingrid and the predicament she'd engineered, but primarily, she realized, out of relief. Water in her hand and cell tucked into her pocket, she unfastened her seatbelt; stepped out of the car and onto the dusty concrete, slamming the door shut behind her.

The Jeep was speeding away before there was time for her to turn around and watch it go.

She exhaled; took a long, slow sip of the water and started to walk, following the path she thought the car had taken. The heat outside was thick: a glutinous, calefying wall of pressure beating down on her from every direction, bringing beads of sweat to the surface of her nose and forehead and gumming her t-shirt to the small of her back.

Half a mile, though. She could do that. Even if doing it meant rocking up to Ellacott looking like she'd jumped fully dressed into a neighbor's swimming pool.

The walk itself was dull: exactly as uninspiring as the parched emptiness of the landscape had promised on first glance. She tried not to look at her cell, to do anything that might run the battery down while she still needed it, but concentrated instead on counting cacti, yucca palms... anything and everything she could use as an interval marker, if she had to.

She didn't see them, when they came for her - because they moved too fast, maybe, sneaking up on her from behind with the stealth of trained assassins, or just because she was distracted, focused on the desert flora and the sweat running down her face and the last thing Ingrid had said to her, would probably *ever* say to her.

They hadn't used a cloth to the mouth and nose to subdue her, that first time; had stuck a loaded syringe into her neck instead, the speed of that action so rapid that her last thought, before she blacked out, was that a mosquito must have bitten her, and that it better not have given her dengue or chikungunya or West Nile virus.

She woke up in agony: a blinding pain so absolute and all-encompassing that it stripped her of any ability she might have had to think, to analyze, to assess what in the hell was happening to her. If she'd had the capacity to translate sensation into cognition and thereafter into language, she might have described the experience as something akin to being torn apart from the inside: as if her bones and tendons and muscles, and the organs they shielded, were being pulled not in four directions but in a hundred, a thousand. As if every component part of her were being separated from every other, with nothing to hold them together but a wafer-thin casing of skin.

It wasn't apparent to her, on first waking, where she was: only that she was horizontal, spread out on a flattened surface of some kind; that she was both unbearably cold and burning hot, and that the sky above her was pitch black and dotted with neon green threads that couldn't have been stars. She had no sense at all of time or how much of it passed as she lay there, but when finally the agony abated - incrementally, like tides receding from the shoreline - and a more tolerable discomfort had taken its place, it was apparent that she wasn't alone: that there were bodies above her, strange-smelling bodies spotted like toads, reaching down to touch her with fingers longer and sharper and crueller than any fingers ought to have been. *Examining* her.

And that she was changed: horribly, irrevocably changed.

CHAPTER 11

The creature was watching her; scrutinizing her as she remembered, like he was scoping out a bug under a microscope.

Her eyes had been closed, as the memories had assailed her: the vivid intensity of what she'd once understood as real impossible to reconcile with the dank strangeness of where she *was*, with the room carved out of rock and the bald, mottled thing that paced it. But now she opened them; now, remembering, she looked out.

"You killed me," she said, as certain of the fact of it as she'd ever been of anything. "You and the rest of them."

"No." The answer came calm, confident and definitive - as if the creature had been expecting to be challenged and had prepared its reply in advance of her asking. "We... improved you. *Augmented* you. We're the reason you're here today, having this conversation. Absent our intervention, you'd have been returned to the soil a very, very long time ago."

"How long?"

The impressions, the recollections... they were fragmented, still - but were *there* now, back in her head, where they ought to have been all along. Or a lot of them were. Not all of them were in sequence, though; in what she felt must be the right chronological order. And her sense of time, *human* time - it felt looser, somehow. Baggier. Neither as linear nor as binding as it had, before.

"How long?" The creature hesitated. Not, she thought, because of any lack of surety on *its* part - but rather, or so it seemed to her, because it was weighing up how best to frame its response. How best to broach the news it had to break. "I'd have to consult the annals, to be absolutely definitive. But three hundred and eleven years, or somewhere close to that, would be my estimate."

Instinctively it struck her as impossible, that so much time - not years but centuries - had passed since Ingrid left her by the side of the road in the desert. But equally, as whatever the creature had given her to drink took root inside her and the remembrances danced and tumbled and slotted themselves into place behind her eyes, she knew - as well as she knew now where she'd gone to high school, and the name of the street she'd grown up on, and how she'd fallen down from her skateboard and broken her wrist the day before her fourteenth birthday - that it was true; that the creature was telling her nothing but the facts of the matter, insofar as it understood them.

And the moment of her death... she remembered that, too. Could feel the fingertips of the cloaked and mottled figures gathered around her: touching her, anointing her all over with a greasy, viscid liquid that smelled like geranium and burned as it touched her skin. Could see herself - herself as she'd been then, the day she'd been snatched from the road on her way to Ellacott - arched and screaming on the same stone table as the boy she'd flashed back to at the Assembly; see herself praying to the God she'd never believed in for an end as the pain shot through her, the *tearing*, and sent every solitary cell in her body into magnesium-white suffering.

The moment of her death - and after.

She'd probably never know what happened to her in the minutes - the hours, even - between her heart stopping, the cessation of her vital functions, and her waking, cold and naked and blighted with tender red scars on a straw-stuffed bed in a room brightened by nothing but moss-light. Where the part of her that her mother would probably have called her immortal soul had gone, if it had gone anywhere.

But the immediate aftermath of her waking, there and then - *that*, she remembered.

She hadn't been alone. Sitting across from where she lay, its thin legs crossed under its brown robe, there'd been another of the creatures, this one more slender and somehow more delicate-looking than the others she'd seen chanting above her as she'd died: its cheekbones more pronounced, its black eyes rounder and wider, its bald head very slightly more shapely. More... elegant, if the word could be applied to whatever manner of thing it was.

"Can you speak?" it had asked her, without preamble, in an English-accented voice that made her think of the kind of clipped, stiff-upper-lipped British actors her grandparents might have listened to in radio plays during the war.

"Yeah," she'd rasped back, surprising herself. Her throat had stung, and her tongue was bone-dry against her palate, but the croak she'd made had been satisfying in a way she couldn't quite articulate even to herself. Had felt almost like an achievement: proof that her body could still be bent to her will, could still be made to do what she demanded of it.

"Good." The creature had crossed and recrossed its legs - reminding Sasha, grotesquely, of a movie *femme fatale*, of Barbara Stanwyck in Double Indemnity and Kathleen Turner in Body Heat and Linda Fiorentino in The Last Seduction - and rearranged its wide, hinged mouth into the semblance of a smile. "You'll have questions, no doubt, and I'd think it would be terribly frustrating for you, if you couldn't give them form."

"What did you do to me? How am I... here?"

What she'd meant, of course, was: *how am I alive? How did you bring me back?*

And the creature had responded as if this was what she'd said aloud; as if it knew exactly what she'd *wanted* to ask but couldn't.

Maybe it had.

"We're less interested in the *how*," another shift of position; another crossing and recrossing of its legs, "than in the *why*. You couldn't possibly know this, of course, but you're rather unusual. Rather special."

Somehow, Sasha had found the strength to sit upright; to prop herself up on her elbows on the mattress.

"What the fuck does *that* mean, *special*?"

The creature had started in its carved stone seat, its already wide eyes widening further - apparently shocked by the profanity.

"Special, Sasha," it had repeated, once it had composed itself. "Unlike anything we've known before."

"My name. How do you know my name?"

The creature had reached into the folds of its robe, into what might have been a pocket, and withdrawn a rectangular strip of plastic that Sasha had clearly recognized, even without her glasses, as her driver's license.

She'd been too preoccupied, in the moment, to fully appreciate the implications of this detail. To ask herself how it was that, after a lifetime of near-sightedness, she'd been able to zoom in on the tiny photograph of her own face on the license with 20/20 acuity - though she'd think about it afterward, and often.

"There's been some conjecture," the creature had said thoughtfully, half to itself, "that it might be your sex. We've tended towards males in the past - they're so very much more inclined to go wandering alone, although I suppose it was ever thus. *Could* it be, perhaps? Might the female body be more robust than the male? Better equipped to manage its own pain without succumbing to it?"

Later, Sasha had wondered something similar herself; had speculated that there might have been some biological basis, some *genetic* basis to her having survived, where the men and boys - the many, many men and boys - who'd come before her had perished. In all the years she spent underground in the tunnels after what the slender creature and the creatures like her had referred to with a kind of awe-struck reverence as Sasha's *resurrection*, she'd never learned the exact figure; had never been told outright just how many men and boys there'd been, how many of them had died screaming in their variation on the agonies that had taken hold of her on that stone table. Although she'd seen it happen to more than a few with her own two eyes.

Many; that was all she knew. Maybe too many to count.

Back *then*, though, the creature's theories about *males* and *females* and the relative resilience of their bodies had meant nothing, but had been as bewildering to her instead as her surroundings, as the rank multi-layered stench of mine-gas in the air and the stinging ache like burrowing needles across what felt like every square inch of her skin and the sensation, above all, of her experience of the world around her tightening and sharpening to a whetted point: its shapes and colors clearer, its sounds louder, its taste more complex on her tongue. Her experience of *herself*, too: the rise and fall of the collagen tissue of her lungs in time with her breath, the flow of blood to and from her heart through her veins and arteries, the contraction of muscle in her intestines as they continued to deconstruct and macerate what little food there was left in her to digest.

She could feel her own body working, she'd realized. Feel, and more than that, *understand* how it was functioning; how they actually operated, those multitudinous internal ecosystems she'd relied on unthinkingly to keep her healthy and nourished and mobile, both individually and as a single, synergistic unit. Understand how they'd kept her alive, in all the thirtysomething years she'd made it through so far; how they were right then keeping her... if not *exactly* alive, then sensate and animate. More so, perhaps, than she'd ever been.

"Why?" she'd said - aware of the flow of air through her trachea, the vibrations in her larynx, the interconnected operations of her entire vocal apparatus.

The creature had looked back at her, and smiled, which in the end had been no kind of answer at all.

She'd got to the *why* eventually, of course - how could she not have, living side by side with the creatures for as long as she had, her social status below ground pitched somewhere between prisoner and honored guest, albeit a guest not one of her hosts would ever allow to leave?

It was a struggle now - even with the Lethe water running through her, reactivating every fallow synapse and reviving every dormant memory - to recall exactly how she'd learned what they were doing down there: the two-hundred-strong community of not-quite-people who'd hewn a subterranean village out of a mountain and who called themselves Seekers. To understand what they were trying to achieve by abducting the men and boys - and one very singular girl - from the surrounding desert and bringing them down into the mines to be tortured to the brink of death and beyond.

But she knew, nevertheless.

Frankenstein: that was how she'd thought about it, for much of her time underground. Not the monster so much as the man, flushed and frenziedly cataloging his instruments of life over the stitched-together sinews of the carcass he intended to rebirth. Because that, in the end, was what they wanted, what they'd wanted long before they'd snatched her from the roadside: to resurrect, to breathe life - *perpetual* and unending life - into the un-living.

Except that, unlike Frankenstein, they'd given themselves a running start: taking living subjects - young, healthy, robustly living subjects - and *making* them dead, before they ever tried to bring them back.

The substance of these abortive resurrections - the *how* of them, what Frankenstein himself might have called the metaphysics of the process - felt similarly hazy, at least for now; although she had an idea that it might clarify itself for her, might reveal itself in greater detail as the Lethe water worked its magic on her system.

Though if she'd ever known the greater *why*, the *reason* for these murderous experiments into life and death and un-life and not-death, then they were lost to her, at least temporarily: the apprehension of them just out of reach, somewhere very slightly beyond her mind's grasp.

The creature hovering over her on the table, the doctor-thing in its purple sash, blinked its black shark-eyes at her and politely cleared its throat, the gestures so incontestably human that they made her shudder where she lay.

Ash, she thought its name was. *His* name. They were gendered after all, the things, or so she recollected now: were male and female and neither and both, the organization of their social roles and identities an approximation of the ones she'd known before.

"Three hundred and eleven years," she repeated.

"Or thereabouts, yes."

"And something... *happened*? To the world?"

There was no question that it had. That some event, or perhaps more likely some convergence of events had conspired to reduce what she remembered of California and Nevada and the northern states above them to something closer to a Dust Bowl - scouring them of so many of the technologies and infrastructures she'd depended on before, and turning the landscape to a real-life vision of the Old West facsimile she'd been reminded of when she'd taken her first step out of Ingrid's car and into the nightmare that had taken root around her since.

Just what events they were, she'd *never* known - of this she was certain. Honored guest or prisoner, it hadn't mattered: they hadn't let her leave the tunnels. Had kept her under constant surveillance; given her no opportunity at all to see daylight for herself. And even when, finally, she'd escaped, after however many years or centuries - when the young and nervous creature tasked that month with watching over her had let its guard slip low enough for her to get away - she'd not broken the surface unscathed. Instead, she thought, the blows to the head she'd taken wrestling with the thing, the thing that was really not much more than a child, had very likely contributed to her amnesia - and to the creation of the false memories, the condition Ash had called *confabulation*, that had had her believing she was another kind of person, from another kind of place and time.

"A great many *somethings*," Ash said ruefully. "What did Hemingway say? Gradually, and then suddenly. Though I imagine you felt the changes more acutely up there than the rest of us ever have down here."

She began to feel it returning to her as he spoke: the strength to her muscles, the sharpness to her thoughts. And more than it had been - more, anyway, than she'd known it to be, in the time that she'd been wandering. Because, she registered now, she *was* strong, *was* sharp: stronger and sharper than she'd ever been in life, in her *first* life. Stronger than human, perhaps; stronger, possibly, than Ash, or any of the others like him.

"Will you let me leave this time?" she asked. "Let me go, if I want to?"

He wouldn't; none of them would. She was their special project, their success story - the one attempt at whatever they were trying to achieve with their *resurrections* that had actually come to pass for them.

But she wanted to hear him say it anyway; wanted to hear how he'd frame the justification, how he'd try to sell it to her.

"Why would you want to leave, now you've come back to us?" The words were calm as they left him; nonchalant, even. But his manner was less so, his long hands steepling together at the fingertips in a way that she remembered - now she was beginning to remember *him* – always unwittingly telegraphed his unease, any time he felt uncomfortable. "You came home. You *chose* to come home."

He hesitated, and she heard - outside the room, in a stretch of tunnel she knew now connected Ash's office to the atrium-like area that served as an unofficial meeting-point and informal marketplace for the hive of Seekers - a scuttle and a clatter of footsteps.

"I didn't know what I was coming back to," she said. "I didn't know anything."

More scuttling, more clattering, and an echo of something that might have been a cry reverberating toward her along the stone walls outside. Ash didn't react; seemed not to hear it, loud though it struck her. Were her ears that much more sensitive now? Or was it that she was only now aware of their heightened sensitivity?

Ash laced his fingertips together and regarded her over the top of them - still nervous, she thought, but hiding it a little better than before, keeping a firmer lid on his reactions.

"You have nothing to fear here." He stepped forward, closer to where she lay, and she tensed her thigh and stomach muscles, wondering whether she'd need to spring up at him from the table, lash out at him with her fists and feet and try to fight her way out of the mines a second time. "We want to protect you, Sasha. To care for you. *Understand* you."

And deconstruct me, she thought. *Pin me down like a frog in a freshman biology class and dissect the parts, even if only figuratively. That's what you mean by* understand, *isn't it?*

The noise outside grew louder, and this time Ash *did* hear it, jumping back from the table in alarm at what was undeniably shouting: raised voices, very possibly in distress.

There was something like a crack that she guessed must have come from the heavy, closed door behind her that separated inside from out, and Sasha bolted up - seizing the chance to slide down to the floor and rise to standing as Ash took two more steps away from the table, virtually backing away from her, or from whatever was going on behind her that she couldn't see.

The crack came again, thunderously loud, and then an ear-ringing crash that Sasha took to be the door coming away from the hinges that held it in place.

She turned her face toward it, and momentarily away from Ash.

She'd been right, she saw: the door *had* broken free of its joints, and now rested on the ground in a bed of dust and splinters. Broken free to show Jess in the hole it had left: her skin lit from underneath by a blacklight glow, a pair of dark wings that might have been cut from shadow unfolding from her shoulder blades, and a look on her face like the wrath of God itself.

CHAPTER 12

A scraping, scrambling noise from behind her pushed her to spin around again, to drag her gaze away from Jess - or whatever winged and darkly luminescent thing was wearing Jess' skin - and over to Ash.

His back was pressed against the wall, his long amphibian fingers digging into the stone and his black eyes widened in fear as they locked on Jess.

He was terrified, Sasha realized. Terrified of *her* - and of what she might do to him.

And maybe his terror was justified, she considered, as she turned back to where Jess stood in the blasted remains of the doorway - *her* eyes blazing gradients of gold from pupil to lid, and a shifting, iridescent halo radiating three inches out from her body.

Her body, and her wings.

They were enormous, the wings: reaching above her head and at least three feet outward on either side of her shoulders. They were darker than pitch, darker than night, but feathered, each quill tapering to a clip-point as sharp as a blade's. The wings of a thunderbird, Sasha thought; of a Garuda.

She didn't speak to Ash directly, though her eyes stayed on him, burning into him so ferociously that Sasha was sure she could feel the air between them sear and swelter, see the particles swirling and vibrating as they heated.

"You ready to go?" she asked Sasha instead, and the voice was the same, was the one Sasha had gotten used to hearing chatter at her over breakfast, shout instructions at her in the garden, call her name in bed, but there was more to it now, too - a gravitas, an age that hadn't been there before. Like an old *grande dame* on Broadway who could still sound young for a part, when she needed to; like the vocals of a song, overlaid onto a saturated soundscape that was only partway audible to the naked ear.

She reached an open, glowing palm out toward Sasha, and Sasha took it without thinking - the fingers burning hers on contact, then settling, until the pressure there was only warm, and no longer painful.

And, hand in hand, they stepped out into the tunnels.

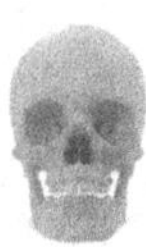

"What do you want to know about first?" Jess said, laying her own, just-made cup of coffee down on the dinner table opposite Sasha's. They were the first words she'd spoken since they'd left the desert, Jess' wings retracted - somehow - into her flesh and Sasha clinging, still weak, to her waist on the back of the oddly striped, high-maned horse they'd found waiting for them at the mine exit.

It was a straightforward question, and Sasha appreciated that; she didn't think she'd have dealt all that well with equivocation or prevarication, in her current state of mind. In her current state of being, perhaps.

And maybe that was as good a place to start as any: the revelation of who Sasha was, or who she'd become, and whether or not Jess knew anything about that. Whether or not she'd known anything about that all along.

Because it struck Sasha now, looking at Jess from across the scarred stretch of wood, that a person - if *person* was even the right designation anymore - who could cow an entire underground city of Seekers into submission through nothing more than her physical presence might also be privy to information she'd yet to disclose *about* that city and *about* those Seekers. And maybe, by extension, about Sasha too.

"You want to go to the mines?" she'd asked Sasha, weeks earlier – a minute before she'd launched into her story about the body in the desert and the Sheriff's Deputy that Sasha was sure now, true though certain parts of it might have been, was only the tip of that particular iceberg. "You sure about that?"

She really *had* been trying to put Sasha off going – that much was obvious now. Put her off by any means she considered necessary, even if that meant pretending ignorance of something she evidently knew more than a little about, after all.

"Me." Sasha took a sip of her coffee: savoured the acidity of the soil below the bitter richness of the beans, the whey and the sugars in the milk, at once repulsed and delighted by the amplification of her senses and the ever-expanding shape of her perceptual world. "Tell me about me."

"What about you?"

"You know what they did to me down there? What they turned me into?"

Jess nodded; didn't hesitate. Her skin was still glowing faintly, Sasha noticed, even in the absence of the iridescent halo, and a gold tinge remained around her pupils. Had it been there before, the whole time - while Sasha had forgotten how to see, how to really *see*?

"Not for sure. But I had an idea. I knew you were..."

"Dead?"

"Not dead." Jess shook her head dismissively at the suggestion. "That's not what I'd call it, not at all."

"What *would* you call it, then?"

"Would you believe me if I said I didn't have a term for it? Can't say I've ever really needed one, before right now. Just... *back*, I guess?"

Sasha mulled it over; tasted the flavor of *back*, the tang and heft of it on her tongue, and found she didn't hate it, after all.

"And you knew," she said. "That that was... what I was."

"Yes."

"How?"

"Well, now." Jess rubbed a palm to the back of her neck - a gesture Sasha would have read, even a day earlier, as a sign of awkwardness, of mild embarrassment. "That question - it might be a little bigger than the one you thought you were asking, there. Though perhaps it's just as well we've gotten to it early on, at that, if you're gonna understand... well, anything at all. See, you maybe think you're just asking how I *know* - about you, about what *you* are. But what you're really asking is: what am *I*, that I should be *able* to know?"

It's like a riddle, Sasha thought. *What has wings, glows black-gold and stops monsters in their tracks just by* looking *at them?*

"Only..." Jess paused. "Maybe that's *not* the best place to start from, after all. Maybe the middle of things is where we ought to be, to begin with."

"The middle of things?"

"You'd probably *call* it the start. But for me..." She trailed off, seemingly lost for a beat in rumination. "Anyhow. Let's start from there, shall we?"

"From where?" Sasha asked - more baffled than irked by the circumlocution, at least for now, but feeling the hot scratch of irritation beginning to build at the base of her skull.

"From *them*. From Pearl, and her... expedition."

She said this as if expecting Sasha to understand immediately who she meant, who *Pearl* was and what the hell kind of *expedition* she was involved with, and Sasha's initial response was impatience: frustration at what felt more and more like needlessly loquacious obfuscation, at the assumption that Sasha *would* understand, that she *wouldn't* need an explanation or a frame of reference.

Was it possible, though, that she *did* understand, or understand something of what Jess was saying, now the fuller reach of her faculties was returning to her? That the name Pearl maybe *did* mean something to her, at that?

Her thoughts shifted quickly, more quickly than the firing of her cylinders had ever allowed them to in life, in the life she'd had before. From doubt to surety to absolute conviction, and immediately thereafter to a face: the slim, high-cheekboned creature with the movie star posture and the cod-British accent who'd been the first to greet her down in the mines, after the change. After the pain of it had begun to subside.

Pearl.

It was right, she knew; was the appropriate name for the face, the correct one, even if she hadn't clawed back quite enough of what she'd lost yet to say *why* that was so.

"Pearl," she said, trying it out aloud for size and discovering that it fit. "*Pearl*. What about it - about *her*? What did she do?"

Jess chuckled, quite unexpectedly: a peal of laughter free enough of rancor to have Sasha believe that it wasn't intended as mockery.

"Oh, darlin'," she answered, the laughter fading to a sardonic smile. "What *didn't* she?"

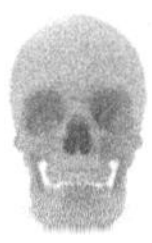

The Egyptology renaissance was still very much in vogue in the London society circles Pearl Harding moved in, eleven years on from Howard Carter's discovery of the tomb of Tutankhamun back in '22. And Britain remained very firmly in thrall to the arcane exoticism of the ancient world, as Carter and the European grave-disturbers who'd gone before him had imagined it.

Like so many of her friends and associates, the bored young women waiting to be married and equally bored young men yet to decide whether to strike out on their own or take up their place in the family business, Pearl was in the market for distraction - distraction, and adventure.

Unlike those of her friends and associates, though, Pearl's enthusiasms alighted not on the history of the ancient world, but on its mythology, and specifically on the Duat: the realm of the dead, as the Egyptians imagined it.

"She read everything," Jess said wearily, as if the very thought of Pearl were a drain on her mental energy. "Cover to cover. All the sacred materials she could buy in translation, or fragments of 'em, and not just the funerary texts y'all have heard of - the Books of the Dead, and those other big hitters. Got real fixated on 'em, too. Even took a couple trips out to the Valley of the Kings, to see what she could find for herself. Got to believin' eventually that it was real - all the stuff she read, all the stories she heard about the underworld."

It was widely assumed, by those familiar with the texts in question, that the Egyptians conceived of the Duat as a physical and not just a metaphorical space - one accessed via the burial chambers that served as portals, as points of ingress and egress both for the bodies and souls of the deceased and for the gods, minor deities and gatekeepers charged with policing the threshold between life and death. It was similarly assumed, moreover, that these portals were located exclusively in North Africa, across the settled lands that followed the flow of the Nile.

Pearl, however, took a different view.

"It made no sense to anyone who knew or cared about Egyptian myth. Damned if I know who it was she talked to that gave her the idea. But she got it into her head that there were *other* portals, outside of Egypt. Outside of Africa, even. And that one of those others was... well, here. Right here, in the Spring - or what *became* the Spring, eventually. Deep down, under the desert."

This last point made no sense to Sasha, either.

"The mines didn't exist back then, surely?"

"The mines... no." Jess grimaced. "But some of the tunnels the mines feed into... *they* were there. They've been there... pretty much always."

Sasha flashed back to the mines, to the phosphorescent trails lighting up the stone-walled tunnels of the underground city that had been her prison, and felt an involuntary shiver pass over her skin.

As readily dismissed as Pearl's claims were by the serious Egyptologists she spoke with, the archaeologists and college professors and hardened ex-military tomb raiders, they nevertheless succeeded in attracting some attention elsewhere: among the cultists and the conspiracists, the lonely and the vulnerable, the believers in Atlantis and the devotees of Fort and Gerald Massey, who together flocked in droves to her Fitzrovia apartment to hear her expound, often at length, on her ever-evolving Great Theory of the New World portal in the desert.

It was only a matter of time before the group - whom Pearl, with an unerring instinct for the value of nomenclature in fostering collective identity, had come early on to dub The Seekers - decided on a field trip across the Atlantic, with a view to exploring the site first-hand and discovering for themselves its manifold wonders. The trip was funded not by Pearl herself, though she could certainly have afforded it, but by several of her more zealous followers, with the largest of the donations coming from the Belgian former doctor who served informally as her second-in-command. The doctor, a general practitioner who went only by the mononym Ash, was viewed with something like suspicion even among his fellow Seekers: his furtive manner, and the quietly whispered rumors around why he might have lost his license back home inducing many of them to take steps to avoid being alone in his company, even for the shortest of spells.

"And they did it, these Seekers," said Sasha flatly. "They went looking. Looking here."

"Oh, yeah. Must have been... 1934, or somewhere close to it. Not quite before Hitler, but long before the name had much currency for many of the folks in these parts."

She sounded a little sad now, Sasha thought; sad and resigned.

"There were nearly two dozen of them, altogether: Pearl and Ash and a bunch of others who could get away with leaving their jobs and their families for weeks at a time on a whim. They rocked up at the Spring one morning in July that year, Kentucky Saddlers kicking up dust at the front of a convoy of wagons so new you could smell the paint coming off 'em. They were perfectly polite, didn't say a word out of place, but there was something *off* about them, you know? And the folks who were living up there then - they knew it. Gave 'em a hell of a wide berth. Old Pearl must've asked half the town for directions to the right patch of desert before she found someone willing to talk to her."

"Sounds almost like you were there."

Jess shrugged - the action as noncommittal as any Sasha had seen her make.

Was it possible, she wondered, that Jess *had* been there, then? That she'd witnessed the Seekers roll into the Spring first-hand, maybe even spoken to them, what must have been - she calculated - near-on four hundred years ago?

And what in the hell must have happened to *them*, between then and now, to transmute them from what she presumed must have been ordinary-looking men and women into whatever they were now - whatever they hell they'd *been* since at least the day they took Sasha?

"What then?" she asked. "Assuming they made it out to the mines - what then?"

Another shrug, another grimace, and Jess' features - her lips, her nose, the eyes that Sasha had spent God only knew how long staring at these last few weeks but never really seeing - contorted into an expression of barely suppressed anger that struck Sasha as a muted shadow of the look she'd worn when she'd first appeared in the blasted doorway of Ash's office, wings spread and pupils blazing.

"Then? They dug. Evidently, they'd brought some manner of excavating equipment with them in a couple of the wagons - picks and shovels and pressure sprays, that kinda thing. It wouldn't have taken much to get down underground, though. Like I said, the tunnels... they were there already. Just waiting to be found."

Quite what Pearl and her Seekers expected to find down there - how they anticipated the underworld would look, from the standpoint of the living - was never documented.

What they stumbled upon, however - after weeks of digging and excavating, searching and Seeking - was a physical terrain not unlike the one described in the recorded myth-scape of Ancient Egypt, and in its Greek and Roman and Mesopotamian equivalents.

A river.

"It looked pretty ordinary, to them anyways," Jess continued. "No licking flames, no rotting corpses, no boatman with a pocketful of coins. Just another underground body of water, not so different on the surface than the Mojave or the Cross Cave out in Central Europe. Only trouble was, they couldn't see a way to cross it - not without a raft or a boat. And not even Pearl thought to bring one of *those* with them."

They made a plan: to leave the mines, head back into town and see what they could buy or beg for that might be fashioned into something sturdy enough to get them across the river.

Except, before they left, they drank from it. Every one of them.

"I'd love to tell you it was out of necessity." Jess stared down into her cup; melancholic now, regretful. "And there could've been a touch of that, I guess. They were down there a while, and maybe their canteens were starting to run dry by then, I don't know. And like I said - it looked like ordinary water, clean enough to be potable. Better than some of the creek water you find up near the Spring, that's for sure."

"I doubt it, though. Knowing Pearl, there'd have been some ritualistic element to it, something she'd have foisted on the rest of the gang. *Imbibing deep of the essence of the dead*, that kinda thing." She laughed aloud at this, at the absurdity of it, the pomposity, and Sasha very nearly laughed with her - a newly hardened part of her softening, just a little, as she remembered how often Jess had made her smile in the weeks before, even when smiling had seemed a dim impossibility.

"It happened right away, the change in them - within the hour. The *visible* change, anyway. There were other things they must've noticed later - the longevity, say. It's been a long time, a *long* time, since they cut a hole in the ground to get into those tunnels, and I'm not sure any one of them has aged even a day since. But then..."

Their hair went first: falling from their scalps into their panicked hands, shedding in clumps and tufts until they were bald as new-born infants. Then their teeth - loosened and forced out of their sockets by the rows of alligator fangs growing in the gums behind them. The skin was next, Caucasian pink giving way to bleached white and spots of fungal green with the consistency of parchment. Finally, the skeletal structure - this last change eliciting screams of agony even from Pearl herself as her spine bent and her limbs lengthened and the bones in her jaw relaxed and dislocated.

"It was horrible to watch," Jess said, gold eyes still fixed to her coffee. "Just horrible. I've no love for Pearl, nor any of them, not after what they've done - hell, what they've done to *you*. But that... I wouldn't wish that on anyone. Not even her."

"Almost sounds like you were there," Sasha observed - the thought she'd been stewing on since that first mention of the Seekers at the Spring now slipping out of her mouth, more or less unbidden.

Jess raised her head; looked Sasha dead in the eye across the table.

"I guess it does. I guess it does, at that. Which takes us right on back to where we started from, doesn't it?"

"Does it?"

"Yeah. That's the thing, you see - I *was* there. Or I should've been. Who'd you think was meant to be keeping watch over the river?"

CHAPTER 13

She'd been called a lot of different names in a lot of different places: none of them ever quite right, but some of them close enough for comfort. To the Egyptians, she was The Hidden Goddess - a sobriquet she took to, because the grandiloquence of it made her smile, and her smiles in those days were rather fewer and farther between than they would be later.

Geography was meaningless to her then, as irrelevant to her as the calendars the humans she observed were beginning to devise to mark the passage of their time. The changing landscapes above her she navigated by their relation to her home, her birthplace - the underrealm those same Egyptians had begun to think of as the Duat. She understood the topographical arrangements of the living primarily in terms of how near or far whatever place she occupied lay in relation to each of the gateways - the ones that would lead her and the dead she accompanied, without fail, back Below.

In the beginning, when the human world was new and her own corporeality a novelty, she flitted, moving from point to point as the mood took her, reporting to no-one and nothing, and always with Ptah's tacit assent - *his* name, at least, the Egyptians had got right. And around her and above her and adjacent to her, that world grew - paradoxically - bigger and smaller by turns, its populations expanding outward even as the physical space between them contracted.

Then, with no warning at all, Ptah came to her: a voice in her head with a set of instructions, the story it told so concrete, so specific, that it might have happened already. Perhaps, knowing Ptah, it had.

She'd been rootless, before: the purpose she served, her guardianship of the passage, bound to no one point, no one gateway. But hereafter, Ptah said, she'd be tethered, tied to one of the gateways in the desert lands with another of her kind for company: she to guard the gate, to keep watch over it, and he to lead the dead of the deserts across the river and through.

And that tethering - that was her first real introduction to boredom.

There was nothing for her to do in the desert; nothing at all. The other one, her counterpart - he was kept busy, because wherever there were settlements, there were dead to carry out across the water.

But guarding the gate? Guarding it against *what*? There were no intruders; no thieves or inquisitive thrill-seekers, as there might have been at the Necropoli della Banditaccia or the Memphis Necropolis. No-one wanted in; not a single soul.

So she busied herself: learned healing from the medicine men in the settlements around the desert and agriculture from the farmers; borrowed book after book from the vast collection her counterpart had amassed over the previous millennia and read each one cover to cover, soaking up traces of theology, mathematics and political philosophy from every scroll and tablet and leather-bound scrap of parchment she could lay her hands on, in Hebrew and Greek, Sanskrit and Sumerian, Egyptian and Akkadian. The knowledge she acquired served no practical purpose, at first - until, out wandering the plains one warm, still-light evening, she came upon a young girl from a nearby settlement spreadeagled on the sand, alone and in the throes of a difficult and apparently unanticipated labor, and found - with what she'd gleaned from the books, and what restorative power she'd brought with her from Below - that she was able to nurse both the girl and the daughter the girl delivered through the process, leaving both in full and perfect health.

Her reputation spread more rapidly than she might have expected thereafter: the medicine men who'd let her learn from them more inclined than before to recommend their patients pay a visit to her strange brick house when those patients' problems seemed insoluble through more conventional means, and many of the women from the nearest communities dropping by to consult with her on matters of childbirth and, especially, child *prevention*.

Later, when the colonizers arrived from Europe and began to cut their bloody swathe through the deserts, she was called on more and more to treat not only the wounds the colonizers left in the people of the settlements but the diseases they'd carried with them across the ocean and let spread.

Later still, when the colonizers had staked their claim on the land and the settlements she'd known had been reduced to a fraction of the size they'd been before, she found herself assimilated, the *de facto* doctor of what was by then known as Ellacott, and what would eventually become Salvation Spring - the lightness of her hair and the golden glow of her eyes and the bastardized Hebrew name she'd adopted for herself leading the Europeans to believe, to her bemusement, that she was one of them.

In all that time, all those many centuries, she'd been essentially redundant in the role Ptah had assigned her; had resigned herself to remaining so, for as long as he willed it.

Pearl Harding and her Seekers, though, threw *that* plan into disarray.

"I'd stopped watching the gate," she told Sasha, her cheeks flushed with what Sasha read as embarrassment - shame, even. "It seemed so unlikely, you know? That anyone'd even want to get through. But they did. They *did*."

She'd *felt* it, when the first of the Seekers touched the water - felt it like a shockwave passing through her, like electricity crackling under her skin.

And had known immediately what it was, what had happened. What she'd *let* happen.

"I went there," she said. "Went there right away, for all the good it did. They'd drunk it already by then - taken it into themselves. It was already starting to change them, starting to turn 'em into whatever the hell it is they are now."

"You don't *know*?" Sasha asked - aware that there were probably larger questions to address, after the story she'd just heard and the *implications* of that story, but entirely unable to articulate *those* yet. "You don't know what they are?"

(*What went on in the world while you were underground*, she thought, the larger questions nudging at her, crying out for her attention.

What happens to the dead, after they cross the water.

What Ptah is, and what it means that he exists at all).

"Not altogether." Jess looked back at her; held her eye. "There's no precedent for it - what they did, what they've become. No-one's ever gotten through like that before."

Because there was always something to stop them, the thoughts continued, in spite of Sasha's determination to ignore them. *Something, or some*one.

No wonder she's ashamed of herself.

Whatever she *is.*

"The Seekers." Sasha settled on them as a topic, for the time being; on the most pressing of the issues confronting them, the one most pertinent to what *she* was now, to what *she'd* become. "What is it they want? What is it they're trying to do down there, with all those people? With *me*? What's so important about bringing us back?"

Resurrecting us, she added to herself, Pearl's words and Ash's ringing in her ears.

"Now, that?" Jess blinked, slowly, breaking the connection between them. "That's the saddest thing of all of this. 'Cause how it started, all they wanted at first - it was to find a way to cure themselves. To pass for human again."

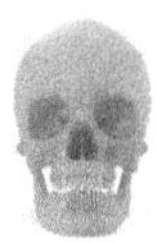

They couldn't leave, after the change; couldn't go back up to the surface. The effects of the water were too great, the physical transformations - both immediate and more subtle - just too extreme. They'd never again be taken for normal, for anything other than monstrous, demonic. They'd have no choice but to conceal themselves; to hide away.

The tunnels were warm enough, and dry. Their supplies had dwindled since they'd bored their way underground, but they were clever, resourceful - more than smart enough to venture out by cover of darkness to steal what they needed to survive from the Spring and its neighboring townships.

But it was no kind of life, not really - not compared to the way they'd lived before.

It was Pearl, of course, who proposed the first solution: a way for all of them to free themselves from their predicament, to wrest back some modicum of control from the universe that had damned them.

There was power beyond the gateway, she told the other Seekers: enormous power, a wellspring of it, power that might well be the very source of life and death itself. She'd read about it; seen allusive references to it scattered through the material she'd come across in the homes of the private collectors she'd known in New York and Chicago, Paris and Berlin.

"Though how in the *hell* she knew to tap into it, I don't know," Jess said. "Whatever rituals she'd seen or read about or had someone recite back at her over cocktails... *I'd* never heard of them. So how *she* could have..."

Of course *you didn't know about them*, Sasha thought - wondering, with a kind of detachment, how someone so very old and so very powerful could be so utterly oblivious to a point so obvious. *You never* needed *to know. Whatever power there was - it belonged to you already. It was part of you; probably still is.*

"Why the murders?" she asked - aware even as she said it that *murders* probably wasn't the right word at all for what the Seekers thought they were doing down there.

"Practice," Jess told her, flatly. "All of them... just practice."

CHAPTER 14

Before

"There are words," Pearl told the others - a new lisp, the consequence of the strange shark-teeth that had grown up through her gums in place of her own, softening her speech and leaving the corners of her now too-wide mouth wet with dark saliva. "Incantations. Ways to draw the power from the river, from *beyond* the river. From the Duat itself."

"What words?" Ash asked, his own tongue tripping and tangling over the plosives, the moist alliteration. He sounded, to Jess - watching and listening intently from a shadowed corner of the cave in which the Seekers had chosen to bed down, so unobtrusively she might have been a part of the rock herself - as if he were chewing on wire; as if his palatal tissues had been ripped to shreds, leaving thickening blood to pool in the pouches of his cheeks.

Pearl shook her head at him, her reconfigured face a mask.

"What *power*?" This was from another of the Seekers - one bulkier and squarer about the jowls than some of his compatriots, though the physical differences between them now were so small as to be negligible. To the human eye, Jess suspected - should any human eye be unlucky enough to alight on them above ground - they'd appear virtually indistinguishable from one another.

Of *this* question, at least, Pearl seemed to be approve.

"The power to heal," she said. "To repair. To... resurrect." She stopped; hesitated. Her orator's pause cast what seemed, to Jess, a kind of spell over her audience - a poor man's simulacrum of the kind Jess had witnessed in Galilee and Athens and at the Temple of Jupiter, before Ptah had brought her out here to the desert. "The underworld, the energy it generates - it's bilateral. Bidirectional. Or it *can* be. We know, we *all* know that it flows downwards - from the living world to the land of the dead, with the passing of souls from one to the other. But it can flow upwards, too - from *them* to *us*. It disanimates, we've seen that; draws the life from the body, the vessel. But it can *animate*, too. *Breathe* life, not only take it."

A feeling Jess had come to recognise since the arrival of the Seekers as concern - as *alarm* - had flooded through her; a second, the closest she'd ever come to panic in what she was beginning to conceive of as her *life* in the desert, following immediately on its heels. There was no precedent for what Pearl seemed to be proposing, that she knew of: not even the Egyptians, obsessive though they'd been about death and the Duat and the rituals they'd practiced in the service of both, had tried to strip the power *from* them for their own ends. Never once had she considered that anyone might.

"Is that... safe?" a third, likely-female Seeker queried, in what reached Jess' ears as a skittish, querulous, British-accented mumble - the not-quite-woman's voice a piccolo played through a mouthful of plums. "I mean... given what's happened already? To, that is to say... us?"

A ripple of perturbation ruffled the mask Pearl wore - then settled, and was gone.

"Rosalind, dear," she said, "you needn't worry. Not one bit. I'd never advocate we try it on *ourselves* before we'd... seen its effects play out elsewhere..."

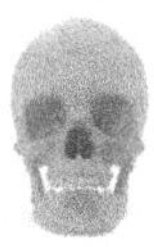

"They're experiments?" Sasha said - barely needing to hear the answer to know it was true. "All those people, those men. *Me.* It's all just Pearl trying to figure out how to turn her people back into real boys?"

"No." Jess bit her lip - with teeth that Sasha saw now were that bit too straight, that bit too perfect to be real, to be something any woman could be born with - and for a second Sasha wanted to reach for her across the table. To take her hand and tell her everything would be okay, however much of a lie that might've been. "It started out that way for them, I guess, but they've got bigger plans now. Bigger ambitions."

"Resurrection not good enough for them?"

She'd been joking, sort of. Trying to inject a little dark humor into the conversation - for the sake of her own sanity, if nothing else. But Jess reacted as if she'd been entirely serious; as if the question had been asked in earnest.

"Enough? Nothing like, not anymore. Not now they think they might've found a way to live forever."

It was the immortality they wanted now, Jess told her. Not the resurrection; not the restoration of life but its perpetuation, its elongation *ad infinitum*, and in a fuller and more satisfying form than the near-on everlasting half-life with which they'd been burdened.

Hence, the men. Hence, the bodies: the skin and bone and muscle torn to pieces on the table that really *was*, in the end, a sacrificial altar.

"They couldn't take it," Jess said, the golden glow around her irises darkening to copper. "Weren't strong enough to hold the power, to keep upright and breathing with whatever current Pearl seems to think she's harnessed flowing through 'em. And why should they have been? They were only human. Only children."

In her mind's eye, Sasha saw the boy she'd hit upon in the desert - bugs swarming from his lips and guts, stalks of alien fungus bursting outward through his orbital sockets and an orchid reaching up toward the sun from the hole in his chest - and wondered what in the hell kind of power, the hell kind of *energy* would do that to a body.

Wondered how in the hell *she'd* managed to survive it. To contain it.

"I don't know," Jess answered, addressing the thought Sasha was *sure* she hadn't spoken aloud. "Why *you* could take it, how you were strong enough... I don't know."

"But I could."

"You could." Jess looked up and over at Sasha from across the table; smiled, strange and sad and rueful. "And darlin' - happy as I am about that, I gotta tell you... that has *not* made my life easier."

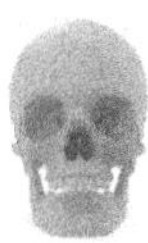

Destabilizing.

Of all the human language she'd acquired, all the English idioms she'd heard develop since the Europeans made their entrance, this one felt to her like the most accurate, the most apropos.

Every time the Seekers took a life, she felt it - felt the shockwaves running through the body Ptah had given her like an earthquake, like a rupture in the veins. It wasn't, she understood almost from the beginning, the taking of the life itself that did this. Rather, it was the ritual, the liturgy - the *words* the Seekers used to wrench the power from the river, from Below, and to direct it through their fingertips into the broken, dying tissues of the men they snatched, the boys.

With every theft, the river trembled - just a little, so little not even Ptah himself might have taken note of the trembling - and then stilled again, its equilibrium restored.

Until one day, it didn't.

"It was you," Jess said simply. "What they'd been trying to do... it never took. You know that now, if you've got your memory back. But with you, for whatever reason... it *did* take. The river, the Below - they channeled it through you, *into* you, but it didn't tear you apart, the way it did the others. It made you stronger. Made you... something else. And the feel of it happening damn near shredded me. Damn near shredded *both* of us."

Her counterpart felt it too, this time - the one who'd been sent with her to the desert in a body of his own. Fearful of his reaction, of *Ptah's* reaction, she'd decided early on not to let him in on what she knew Pearl, about the Seekers; to keep him in the dark. He, therefore, had been entirely perplexed by the physical sensations that had overcome him, in the moments of Sasha's change.

"He's connected to the river," she continued. "To the river and Below, just like I am. They run through us. Same way that now, I guess... a little of them run through *you*, too."

She'd confessed, when he'd come to her; confessed everything. About Pearl and the Seekers: what they'd done, and what they'd become; what they intended to do, and what they might finally have succeeded in doing. Confessed her own culpability; her own negligence.

"He wasn't happy. Wasn't happy at all. Said I should've told him sooner - told him when the whole thing started. That me not telling him made him vulnerable, made all of us vulnerable. And he was right. What Pearl and her friends are doing, the way they're playing with that... what would you call it? That power? That energy? It could be the end of us. Of all of us."

Sasha processed things more quickly now, more efficiently: her thoughts coming clearer and faster and her intuitions crystallizing into knowledge more reliably than they ever had in her first life, her *real* life. She was pretty sure she knew what Jess was getting at - what kind of danger the Seekers represented to the river and the Duat and to Jess herself. But she wanted to hear her *say* it, so she pushed for the details anyways.

"The end of who?" She fixed Jess' sunglow eyes with a stare of her own; gave her no chance at all to look away. "Which *us* are we talking about here?"

Jess gave another of her sad smiles, to Sasha's surprise - the kind of smile, it occurred to Sasha later, that you might offer the family dog, just before you took it to the vet's office to be put to sleep.

"You really telling me you haven't worked it out? I find that a little hard to believe, if you don't mind me sayin'. But alright - I'll play along. All of us, is who. Every single, solitary creature left alive in this smoking crater of a world you people made for yourselves."

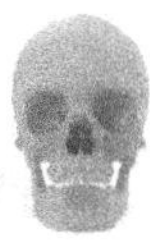

The borders were porous, at the gateways - those fissures Ptah had allowed into the fabric of things, to separate the realms of the living from Below. They had to be - how else, after all, could the souls of the dead move from one to the other, across the river?

But the movement between them... whatever Pearl had told her acolytes, it *wasn't* bidirectional. The traffic had only ever flowed one way: *from* the living world, *to* Below.

This was logical; coherent. It was how Ptah had willed it, when he'd ordered the structure of the universe.

Porous borders, but borders that *held*.

The attempts the Seekers made to siphon off the energy - the life-force, the *death*-force - from the Duat... they'd done no real damage, before. The boys had died, their bodies collapsing in on themselves under the weight of a power they hadn't been built to contain - and that power, or so Jess assumed, had simply ebbed away again, and back to the river.

Until Sasha.

"I should've stopped them," Jess said, lost again in her memories. "As soon as they started in on the killings, I should've shut 'em down - ended it, there and then. But they'd drunk the water, you know? There was a connection there, too - to the river, to Ptah. I didn't know how it would go, if I tried to break that. What effect that might have, what damage it might do. What Ptah might get to hear about it."

"And then... me," Sasha prompted - pulling Jess back to what seemed as if it might be the crucial part of the story, the jigsaw piece that would bring the other, disparate fragments of the puzzle together into a cohesive picture. "What happened, when they brought me back?"

The blast had sent Jess reeling, when it hit; dropped her to her knees, the spikes of pain and nausea - physical sensations for which she'd had no reference point, before - shooting upward from her stomach to her cranium, her bones and teeth conducting the vibrations along her skin in ever-more-sickening oscillations.

He'd been with her when it happened, her counterpart: had fallen to his own knees, pawing at the air around his head with cupped hands as if he were staving off an insect attack.

He'd known, then, what it meant: the pain, the sickness, the sense of something moving and shifting and *loosening* beneath them, of a crack developing in unseen foundations.

Of something stable, beginning to weaken.

Gradually, then suddenly: that was how it went. How everything fell apart.

There were no sudden, seismic shifts, despite what she and her counterpart had felt at the moment of its happening, of the borders between worlds giving way. No skyscrapers fell; no coastal cities collapsed into the sea.

The change took hold far less dramatically; with a lack of spectacle that might even have been disappointing, to an observer with no investment in the outcome. But when it *did* take hold, it bit down: latched on with its teeth, and didn't let go.

The first deaths were reported in Ontario - although there'd been whispers of a rash of similar cases coming out of São Paulo and Kolkata for at least two months before the international press ran the Canadian story. The deceased were an elderly couple, Ruth and Lauren Siegel, and their adult son Augustus - a single, never-married forty-four-year-old accountant who lived quietly at home with his mothers. All three Siegels had died within twenty-four hours of one another, in the same infectious diseases unit of the same hospital in Toronto. All three exhibited identical and equally bewildering symptoms: a lightening and visible decaying of the epidermis, transforming their complexions (Ruth's a pale peach, Lauren's and Augustus' a honey brown) into the same uniform shade of green-tinged white; a softening and dislocating of the jaw and concomitant loss of the dentition; a darkening of the pupils and the sclera, and an erosion of the vertebrae, resulting in a significant and virtually overnight reduction in height. The cause of death of all three was registered as heart failure, although both the medical examiner who conducted the autopsies and the half-dozen colleagues he called in to verify his findings were privately of the belief - given these symptoms - that there were other precipitating factors at work, factors they'd been unable to isolate or identify post-mortem.

Two of these colleagues had already begun to plan the article they'd pitch to the New England Journal of Medicine when the first tidal wave of infection landed, rendering further research into any such article redundant.

A half a million died in the United States alone, those first four weeks: enough to overwhelm every hospital on the Pacific Coast and induce

Governors from thirty-seven out of fifty states to declare a state of emergency and urge the inhabitants of their respective regions to stay indoors with the windows closed, until whatever pathogen was causing their neighbors to rot and shrivel from the inside-out could be identified and contained, if not cured or entirely eradicated.

This advice was largely heeded, but ultimately did no good at all. And by Week Twelve of what was known at the time, in the absence of a better or more accurate term, as necropathy - and more colloquially thereafter, equally inaccurately, as Bone Rot - the governors themselves were dead, along with the vast majority of their voters.

"Three hundred and forty-seven million people," Jess said, her eyes still locked on Sasha's. "That's how many there were in this country. Before."

Don't ask, Sasha told herself. *Don't ask, because she'll tell you. And if she tells you, you'll know, and you'll never* not *know again.*

And you can try all you want to convince yourself that it wasn't your fault - that you *didn't do it, that the Seekers did it* to *you. That it's on them, what happened after. Not on you.*

But how much comfort is that really going to bring you, when it's the middle of the night and you're staring up at the ceiling, counting bodies instead of sheep?

Spin it however you want. Repeat whatever lies you need to in your head and under your breath. But this, all of this... it's because of you.

"And now?" she said - ignoring the voice, pushing down the beginnings of the oil-slick of guilt she suspected she'd never be free of again. "How many are there now? How many are left?"

"For certain? I couldn't say." Jess bit her lip. "There's not been a whole lot of census-taking, since it happened. But if I had to guess, if I had to put a number on it, from the things I've seen? A million, between here and the east coast. A million... maybe less."

CHAPTER 15

Rooster's office smelled like decay - like wet wood and sauerkraut, smoked fish and animal dung.

Rooster himself had, Sasha noticed now, no odor at all: neither the allium tang of underarm sweat that clung to the clothes of the townspeople, nor the freshwater and citrus taste of Jess' skin and hair. The man had no scent, no flavour - and, she realised now, with the acuity of her senses returned to her, made barely a sound as he paced about the sawdust floor, despite the flat-footedness of his stride and the ungainly proportions of his gaunt accordion body. If she closed her eyes, she thought, it might be easy to forget that he was in the room at all.

"You knew that it was her, yet you kept it from me?" It was Jess he was speaking to, not Sasha - Jess, and only Jess. Sasha might as well have been an ornament; a static lamp, or a piece of furniture. "Did you learn nothing at all from the first calamity?"

Both his accent and the patterns of his speech were different than they'd been, or at least they seemed so to Sasha's ears. The dry, droll tone and Old West vernacular were gone now, replaced by something altogether more formal, more statesmanlike and much, much older. It wasn't that he'd deliberately altered the way he spoke, she thought; rather it was that, like Jess, he'd simply elected to let the veil drop, to stop trying to hide himself behind the small-town craftsman guise he'd cultivated.

She'd guessed who Rooster was, without Jess needing to confirm it: that he was the counterpart she'd talked about, the other being Ptah had sent out to the gate in the desert. The one charged with ferrying the dead across the river, to the Duat.

It explained the coded looks and cryptic words Sasha had known to pass between them; the easy sibling-like intimacy that showed itself in wisecracks and help given, and given freely, before it was sought. And what profession would fit a man like that more perfectly than undertaker, if she really stopped to think about it?

"I *didn't* know," Jess said, sounding conversely more like herself than she had, or more like the self she'd shown to Sasha in the beginning: the flesh-and-blood woman who cooked and fought and healed the sick, instead of… whoever or whatever she actually was, under the skin. "And I'm telling you now."

She *had* known before, though, hadn't she? She'd admitted as much. Known something of the truth, if not the whole of it. If not from the moment Sasha walked through her door and stood beside her while she delivered a baby and walked a girl back from the edge of death with nothing more elaborate than a kiss to the forehead, then certainly later. Certainly after the first time Jess had undressed her and taken her into her bed.

"What do you intend to do about it?" Rooster pressed - once again with no acknowledgement at all that Sasha was right there in the room, was standing so close beside Jess that their shoulders were touching.

She was too numb for anger, still - too dazed, after everything she'd learned this last day - but she felt a sting of irritation at the slight nonetheless; a prickle of resentment that might *become* anger, left unchecked.

And maybe Jess sensed it in her, felt Sasha's hackles rising, because the question she asked next was addressed to Sasha, and not to Rooster.

"Would you mind giving us a minute, honey?" She took Sasha's hand and squeezed it - the first sustained physical contact between them since they'd fled the mines. "Me and Rooster, we got a few things to straighten out here."

The dismissal stung too, more than Sasha cared to admit, although the *honey* took some of the bite out of it; she thought Jess probably knew that, and had deployed it to that very end.

"Sure," she said, as indifferently and with as much dignity as she could muster, and stepped out of the office - through the carpentry room next door, where row after row of empty wax-lined coffins jostled for space with rough-cut cedar planks and woodworking tools, and onto the dry almost-twilight of the street outside.

The town was quiet; eerily so. Not a soul was out, that she could see, and no sound traveled from the shuttered windows of the closed-up barrooms and the general store across the way. They weren't night-owls, the people of the Spring - she'd come to realize that early on in her stay. Unless they had a reason to be out later, and a really compelling reason at that - something like the Assembly, say - then every one of them was home with the blinds drawn by seven in the evening, tops, leaving nothing on the street but dust and silence.

It was a different silence than the kind she'd known before, she understood now - now she had a *before* to return to in her memory. Now there was Ingrid, and Aurelia, and her mother, and her old studio by the beach in Santa Monica; now there was a past with more to define it than the presence of scars she couldn't explain and a feeling of dislocation from everything she saw and touched.

What she'd considered silence then really *hadn't* been. There'd always been something, even when she'd been entirely alone, when there'd been no-one else around for miles: the chatter of birds, or the hum of electricity passing through cables overhead or underfoot.

There was none of that here.

Before today - before Ash's Lethe water had disabused her of the fiction that this was *her* world, was the world she'd been born into, and before Jess had filled in the terrible blanks about what happened to that world when Sasha had left it - it hadn't seemed to her particularly strange, this unending absence of background noise.

Now, though - now it choked her. Did nothing but remind her of what ought to have been there, the noise that *ought* to have carried to her on the air even in the quietest of places but that never would again, because of the Seekers and what they'd set loose. Because of *Sasha*, and the price her second life had exacted.

Then, unexpectedly, there was something, after all.

Voices, thick with the heat of an argument - pitched so low she shouldn't, by rights, have been able to hear them. Almost certainly *wouldn't* have been able to hear them, when she'd been nothing but human.

Rooster, and Jess, from all the way inside the office.

"They want her back," he was saying - each syllable a blunt statement of fact, brooking no disagreement. "You've seen this for yourself."

"Yes." Jess sounded more clipped than usual, to Sasha's ears; more abrupt. "Hence my intervention. As I've said."

"They'll try again. You realize this."

"I assumed nothing less. But she's here now, with us. Under our protection."

"Which you seem blithely confident will be sufficient. Need I remind you how many of them there are, now? How greatly they outnumber us?"

"They fear us. Not one of them dared lay a hand on me, in the tunnels."

"Nevertheless, they want her. Perhaps enough to overwhelm that fear."

"Are you suggesting she won't be safe with us?" Jess was angry now, or so Sasha thought; riled up, though her tone was just as hushed as it had been. "With *me*?"

"I'm *suggesting* only that the consequences of their reclaiming her would be ruinous, and that we'd be unwise to take that risk."

"Reclaiming her? She's a living being, not a plot of land."

"*Is* she? I understood that she hadn't been a living *anything* in quite some years."

"Don't be such a goddamn pedant. You know what I mean."

"And *you* know what *I* mean, and you need not pretend otherwise. What has happened once might easily happen again. And were they actually able to study her, as you believe they intended to earlier, and able by some further stroke of fortune to ascertain *how* their... experiment succeeded on her where it's failed so often elsewhere..."

"They won't."

"It isn't possible for you to make that claim with certainty. And so I repeat: were they able to understand how they succeeded with her, and were they able thereafter to replicate that success, perhaps on themselves... it would be cataclysmic. Doing so *once* was enough to bring this world to its knees. I have scarcely the courage to imagine what chaos doing so ten or twenty or a hundred times more might set forth upon what remains of it."

A pause, and a long intake of breath - what Sasha knew to be the sound of Jess reining in her temper.

"That won't happen. I won't allow it to."

"Then you're a fool, and I'd wager that whatever spell this... dalliance has cast on you has *made* you foolish. Has blinded you to what needs to be done."

"And what would that be, now?"

Maybe, Sasha thought later, it was the venom in her words that gave him pause. Or maybe it was simply that he didn't want to say aloud what needed to be said.

Either way, he was kinder, when he spoke again. Gentler, in spite of the content of his speech.

"She shouldn't *be*," he said. "You know that. And for as long as she endures, *we* are imperilled - every one of us, above and Below. For all of our sakes - she must be ended. Ended now, before any further damage can be done."

CHAPTER 16

She ran, before she could hear more.

Jess wanted to protect her, to shelter her from the Seekers - she'd said as much, and Sasha had believed her. But what did that matter, when it was stacked up against what *Rooster* had said - what *Rooster* believed needed to happen, for what was left of the world to be any kind of safe again?

He'd kill Sasha himself, if he had to. She was sure of that much, too.

That the Seekers would be looking for her hadn't come as a surprise. It had been clear enough, back down in the mines - in the caves - that they intended to keep her there: to watch her, study her, try to unlock whatever secrets they thought she held, just as they'd done before her original escape. And she thought that maybe Rooster was right, and they wouldn't stop - not until they got ahold of her again, regardless of whatever obstacles Jess laid in their path.

Which made running, here and now, the best option, didn't it?

They'd come to the Spring by horse, Sasha riding behind Jess on the back of the striped stallion; had left him tied up just outside the town limits, so as not to draw attention to their arrival. Sasha wouldn't try to take him, though, she decided, even as she was sprinting as light-footed as she could away from the undertaker's office: not only because Jess or Rooster or both were likely to pick up on the sound of his hooves, even at a distance, but because she was nearly all the way certain the horse wouldn't *let* himself be ridden. Not by her; not by anyone but Jess.

She ran as fast as the aching muscles in her hips and calves would carry her, the bones of both shins protesting at the sudden acceleration - past the shuttered scattering of stores and homes that together comprised the main drag of the Spring, and back out into the cooling nothingness of the plains.

There was no reason now for going back toward Jess' place, and even less sense in heading out toward the mines, so she took the route she'd arrived by - the one that would lead her back out into the desert, the mile upon mile of rock and cactus and scorpion-riddled sand she'd traveled through on her way to the Spring, to the mines.

She'd had Puppy Dog then, of course; Puppy Dog, and her tent, and enough food and water in her canteen to see her through for days. For weeks, if she was frugal.

She had nothing now. No food, no water, no transport but her own two feet and no means of shielding herself from the bugs or the elements.

How long she'd last out there without these things, with the sun disappearing and solid shadow falling over the desert like a blackout curtain... that, she elected not to dwell on.

When there was no more breath in her lungs and her legs were burning with the effort of exertion, she slowed to a jog, and then to a walk - her ears filled with the hiss of rattlesnakes, the scurrying of spiders and the burrowing of the beetles she knew were all around her, invisible but ever-present, and the occasional anguished canid howl she hoped meant coyotes and not wolves. Her mouth was dry and powdery with grit, but her eyes saw better in the dark now; saw the gnarled outline of every root and the panicles of every patch of brittlebush that were, if not quite enough to navigate by, then at least a sign that she was moving forward, moving *onward*, and not chasing her own tail.

There was something hypnotic about the constituent sounds of the prairie, she thought. Not soothing, not by a long way, but distracting - the constant, dissonant whir and hum of the whole they made giving her a point to fix her mind on that wasn't Jess, or the Seekers, or her own complicity in the destruction of the world, or where the hell she'd actually *go* once she ran out of desert. It took her to a different time, a different place: to the trek she'd tried to make from Ingrid's Jeep to the little town of Ellacott, a bottle of water in her hand and the mixed irritation and relief she'd felt at Ingrid breaking up with her propelling her on to the promise of a hire car and a cell signal.

Perhaps if she'd been less absorbed by the memory, it struck her afterward - less lost in her own reverie - then she might not have fallen again into the same trap she had then. Might have been more attuned to the footsteps of the circle of attackers, as they descended on her from what felt like every corner of the earth; might have bought herself the opportunity to fight or flee, before they seized her.

Before the noose was tight around her neck, and they were dragging her face-down along the desert floor, rope knotted around the knuckles of their green-speckled fingers.

CHAPTER 17

It was Pearl, not Ash, who stood guard over Sasha when she came around - came around naked and sweating, on the same table she'd been laid out on in Ash's ersatz examining room the day before. Her arms were fixed to the stone this time by steel manacles, her ankles bound together with a measure of what felt like the same rough rope the Seekers had used to drag her from the desert to the mines - the skin of her cheeks and chin and forehead scraping red-raw along the hard, sun-baked soil until pain and lack of oxygen had overwhelmed her, and she'd slipped away into unconsciousness.

"Try to get up," Pearl said, as cool as the chain-links pressed to Sasha's wrists, "and it will cost you. Ash may be reluctant to cause you distress when he takes stock of you, but I have no such qualms myself. You will stay still, or you will suffer. These are your choices."

There was a knife in her hand: wide and flared and sharp as a short sword, both the blade and the handle carved from ancient-looking stone. The same stone, perhaps, that lined the walls of the caves. And she'd use it, Sasha thought; use it happily, if she felt she needed to. Whatever reserves of empathy or humanity she'd had when she and her acolytes had first tunneled down into the mine, they were gone now. There was no better nature left to appeal to; no compassion. No understanding of Sasha as something sentient or kindred - as something alive, the same way *Pearl* was alive.

Maybe that's because neither of you are, Sasha heard herself say - the aside, thankfully, uttered only in her head, and not aloud.

"They'll be coming for me," she said, aware as she spoke of both the weakness of the threat and the vagueness of *they* as an identifier. Would Pearl even know which *they* she was talking about? Would she have put two and two together, after Jess' dramatic rescue operation? Connected Sasha with Jess - with Rooster, even?

Did she know who Jess and Rooster *were*, for that matter? Rooster suggested she did - and the other Seekers' cowering reaction to Jess' appearance in their space seemed to confirm as much. But did she know all of it? *How* old Jess and Rooster were, *how* powerful?

"Let them come." Pearl's grip on the knife tightened, sending dark veins pulsing to the surface of her death-white hands. "What harm do you believe that they can do us? Oh, Ash and some of the children may have been... alarmed at first, when your friend made her entrance - they hadn't seen her *quite* like that before, I understand. *Quite* so... unsheathed. But we can't be harmed - not by them. Perhaps not even by Ptah himself. The source of the river runs through us now, through all of us. We can no more be destroyed than can the Duat."

"You can be hurt though, can't you?" Sasha said - the words spilling from her too fast for her to wonder whether needling Pearl was sensible, would serve any purpose that was even in the ballpark of self-preservation. "You can't be ended, maybe - and there's still a question mark over that, the way I heard it - but you can be made to suffer. To feel pain. Could be *that's* what they've got in mind for you - for all of you."

The tip of the knife edged closer to her chest; to the thickened scars that formed a Celtic knot below her breast, over whatever was left of her heart.

"I won't be provoked." Pearl ran the sharpest point of the blade across the skin there - the shallow cut it made smarting and burning and releasing a fine line of red-black blood from Sasha's body. "And I'd remind you that you can *also* be hurt, and far more readily than any one of *us*. So if you're entertaining any thoughts of trying to goad me into killing you quickly, before you've served your purpose... you may want to put them to bed now. Happy though I am to do this, if it keeps you in line," she pressed the tip of the knife very slightly further into Sasha's chest, causing the initial paper-cut sting to blossom into a deeper and more nauseating ache, "you'll be staying alive for us, as long as we need you."

And maybe it was a reasonable assumption, Sasha thought - that she'd *want* Pearl to kill her, and do it fast. Out of altruism, sure: to stop the Seekers using her to release another, greater wave of devastation on the world, *across* worlds, if Pearl even knew that Sasha was aware of that particular consequence. But for more selfish reasons, too. Because there was no chance at all, now they had her back in the tunnels, of the Seekers letting her escape again. And they'd be less gentle in analyzing her, in *deconstructing* her, this time around; in pulling her apart, to uncover her secrets.

A quick death, weighed up against years or decades or even centuries of imprisonment and scrutiny and testing... perhaps it wouldn't be so terrible, after all.

If it were even possible, anymore. If she *could* be killed.

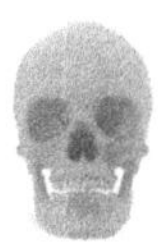

Pearl left her there, strapped to the table - under the wary fish-eyes of not one but three heavy-set, broad-necked Seekers, all of them armed to the teeth with rock-sculpted spears and broadswords, maces and short-handled axes.

They really *wouldn't* let her go again - that much was clear. They'd do whatever it took to keep her.

And Jess and Rooster would come for her - she knew that just as well. Jess because she cared for Sasha, and Rooster because he feared her; or, if not *her* exactly, then what she represented. What she might do; what her body and whatever coursed through it might precipitate, in the Seekers' hands.

Because, in the end, if she *could* be killed, he'd probably kill her himself.

So, she waited.

And eventually, they came.

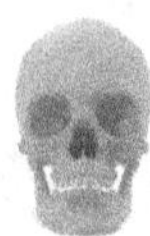

Rooster's wings were smaller than Jess', and pitch-black, the ends of each feather finished with a tarry veneer that made Sasha think of poison-tipped arrows - and which was, she suspected, every bit as dangerous to the things they touched.

Pearl's guards didn't cringe or shake on seeing them burst through the ruined doorway into the office, as Ash had on seeing Jess; were, on the surface, unfazed by their angel's wings and iridescent glow, by the studded flails and sickle-swords they brandished.

Instead, no doubt on Pearl's orders, each guard stood his ground, his own weapons raised in preparation to strike - Sasha's chained, stretched body a barrier between himself and the invaders.

With a little effort, and a little judicious application of the strength she hadn't known she'd had until the previous day, she could free herself, or so she thought; could ball her fingers into fists and shatter the manacles with the clenching of her forearms. She hadn't wanted to try, before; had recognized the futility of performing the gesture in a roomful of unnaturally strong creatures who'd been instructed to detain her at all costs.

Now, though...

Rooster moved first: slid forward toward the biggest of the guards with inhuman speed, his khopesh drawn. The guard was bright though, if not quite as quick; he sidestepped, blocking the blow with the head of his axe, and then closed in on Rooster's left, the other two Seekers following in his wake until Rooster was surrounded.

She felt a pressure on her right arm, the arm she hadn't been working on releasing from the chain; whipped her head around as much as she was able and saw Jess leaning into her, pulling the steel jaws of the other cuff apart with her bare hands.

"You okay?" Jess asked her, as the metal gave and Sasha's hand came loose. "Can you get up?"

Sasha bent her legs experimentally, the rope at her ankles keeping them fastened together - then, happy to find the blood still flowing through the muscles, jerked her knees apart and ripped the rope into two clean pieces.

"I think so," she said. 'Except..."

She gestured down to the other cuff, the one holding her left wrist in place. Jess saw it; nodded and began to steer herself around to the other side of the table.

"Rooster can handle them," she told Sasha, pulling at the left-hand manacle and pointing behind her, where the undertaker and two of the Seeker guards were caught up in the sort of dirty fighting Sasha couldn't help but think of as a skirmish. "Let him keep 'em busy, and you and I can..."

She trailed off mid-sentence, her gold eyes widening and her forehead rearranging itself into a puzzled frown, then lowered her chin to her chest, seeming to consider the front of her body - where, Sasha saw as her own eyes followed, the blade of the third Seeker's sword had torn right through the flesh, back to front.

"What in the...?" Jess started, her face a picture of disbelief - and crumpled to the ground at the feet of the shellshocked-looking guard, his blade still skewering her gut.

It was instinct and not logic that made Sasha cry out for Rooster, her scream threatening to shred the lining of her throat to tatters.

Apparently acting on instincts of his own, Rooster threw a look to Sasha and the table - both of his arms and the razor-tips of his wings engaged in parrying strikes from the remaining Seekers.

He saw Jess on the ground, sticky gold gouts of what could have been blood pouring from the holes cut out of her back and abdomen, and let out a scream of his own: a stream of ululations, punctuated by phrases - that sounded to Sasha very much like pleas - in a language that she'd never heard before.

Whereafter, all sound ceased, and the world went white.

CHAPTER 18

Ptah, Jess had told Sasha earlier that day as they'd sat opposite one another at the kitchen table, was not an interventionist god.

But apparently, from time to time, he made exceptions.

The bent-backed, green-skinned little man who was the first thing Sasha saw when she opened her eyes looked nothing at all like the Creator she'd been taught to worship back in Sunday school, nor anything like the smiling, blue-eyed Savior her mother had prostrated herself before at Mass - though she understood immediately and instinctively that he was every bit as powerful, every bit as transcendent.

Nor did the empty room in which she found herself seem much at all like any Catholic conception of heaven, despite the blinding whiteness of its walls and floor and ceiling, and despite the sensation of absolute blankness that permeated it. Rather, it was as if she'd woken into a void - a pocket of immateriality outside of measurable time and concrete space.

Rooster was there too, she saw, when she pulled her gaze away from the green-skinned man and his dazzling white backdrop: standing equidistant from her and the man, the three of them forming a not-quite-human triangle in the centre of the not-quite-room.

Rooster's wings were spread, just as they'd been in the tunnels, but his clothes were different: the undertaker's get-up that was all she'd ever seen him in replaced with a plain black tunic and a necklace of skulls, each one no bigger than the palm of her hand.

And perhaps *this* was the real him, after all, she thought; *this* was what the dead perceived, when he took them out across the river.

"Rooster," the little man said - though that wasn't the name he used, only the name Sasha heard, just as the language he spoke wasn't English but became so anyway when it landed on her ears, "it's good to see you."

"Lord," Rooster replied, bowing his head in deference - the title delivered in that same language, one she really *shouldn't* have understood.

"You called on me."

"Yes." Rooster raised his head a fraction; enough to look the little man face-on. "For help."

"For help." The little man seemed pensive; bemused.

"This... situation, above. It's gone too far. It must be rectified."

"It *must* be?" There was an edge to the little man's voice at this that might have been admonishment - though it sounded, to Sasha, something more like amusement.

"Please, Lord. They struck her down, the insurrectionists. You must have seen it."

Jess, Sasha thought. Of course, Jess.

The little man hesitated before answering.

"She is hardly ended," he said, and now Sasha imagined she glimpsed a hint of irritation there, an impatience for Rooster's inability to grasp what ought to have been straightforward. "The destruction of the body is not the destruction of *her*. You know this."

"Nevertheless." Rooster drew himself up to his fullest height, until he was towering over the little man before him. He was more than thin and rangy now, Sasha saw - was impossibly tall, a giant, larger by far than any mortal *could* be. "None of this ought to have happened as it did. This world has grown warped, misshapen, and for no reason but the self-interested fumblings of a handful of souls who knew no better. The plagues, and the plagues to come - they're not *human* plagues, Lord. They're of *our* world, not theirs. We have a duty to intercede. To rectify."

He stopped; touched a single skeletal finger to the skulls around his neck and lowered his head back down. He was nervous, Sasha thought; aware, maybe, that he'd overstepped his bounds in making demands.

Ptah's response, however, was thoughtful, even-handed - if not quite, perhaps, what Rooster might have been expecting.

"Tell me, child," the little man said softly, addressing Sasha. "Where do you stand on this? This is *your* world, after all. *Your* business. And there can't be many of your kind left alive with so... direct a connection to this plague that Rooster speaks of."

He means guilt, Sasha told herself. *He's asking how you feel, because you're the thing that* caused *the plague. The one who broke the world.*

"I don't know," she said, answering him as honestly as she knew how. "I didn't see it. They kept me away from it, the Seekers. Underground. I wasn't... there, when it happened."

Ptah nodded, seeming to understand.

He walked across the white room toward her, his gait a sprightlier one than his stooped appearance suggested, and came to a halt immediately in front of her - so near to her face he might have been readying himself to kiss her.

"See, then," he told her, pressing his fingertips against her temples.

And she saw.

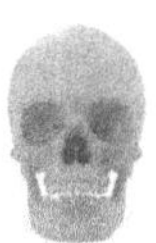

Ingrid had been lucky: there'd still been beds available in the hospital when she was admitted, still drugs enough left in the pharmacies to ease at least a fraction of the pain that tore through her body as her bones began to soften.

She had no visitors, no friend or girlfriend or elderly relative to sit with her at her bedside or bring a glass of water to her lips when she was thirsty - but no-one did, by then. The hospitals were war zones, as chaotic and as dangerous as the streets outside.

She died alone in the middle of the night, her death unregistered until the following morning by the few doctors and nurses who remained.

Still, she'd been lucky.

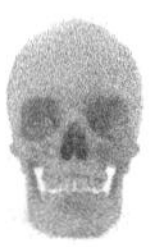

The city was on fire. It might have been L.A., or San Francisco, or somewhere else entirely - who could say, when there was nothing to see but torched cars and burning buildings and the dancing shadows of the fire-starters, cackling maniacally in the reddening darkness?

The power was gone by then, the grid brought down and the stations unmanned. The water would last longer, although that would dry up too, in time.

What survivors there were had yet to leave - but hid, for now, in their unlit apartments and airless basements, waiting for a change in fortune, for *someone* to do *something*.

Eventually, when no-one did, they'd move on.

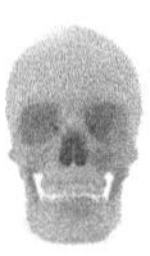

Sasha barely recognized her mother as she lay dying: Marisol's face and body leached of all the color it once had, her limbs contorted under the covers and her toothless mouth caved in on itself.

The priest was with her, in her bedroom: Father Henry, the last of his kind at St. Augustine, possibly the last of his kind in the county, the state.

He didn't speak, or pray over her; just smiled at her, and held her hand in his as she passed.

Closed her eyes for her, after.

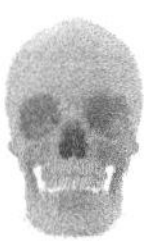

The survivors traveled in packs, when they finally left the cities: in pairs and trios, small groups and larger gangs. There was safety in numbers - in numbers, and in firepower. Every one of them was armed, younger and older alike.

They headed for open space: for the deserts and the mountains, the wetlands and the tundra and the plains. As far away from the cities as the vehicles that they'd marshaled would take them, from the devastation that was all that was left there.

Away from the mayhem, and the rot.

Aurelia died wrapped up in her lover: a modern history professor she'd been seeing only a few months when the necropathy set in.

The lover survived three more days, alone in the house with Aurelia's corpse, before she followed.

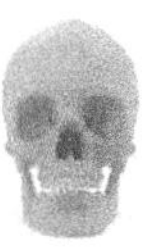

In the deserts and the mountains, the wetlands and the tundra and the plains, the survivors settled; put down the beginnings of what might eventually be roots.

Began the long, slow process of rebuilding.

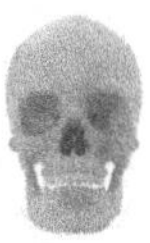

And on the stone floor of Ash's examining room, a blade bisecting her body, Jess looked up at Sasha and tried to speak, but nothing came.

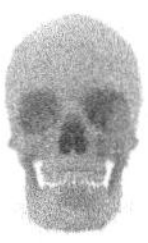

Ptah removed his fingers from her temples, and Sasha's vision cleared.

"What is it you want?" he asked her.

"Not that," she told him, her throat thick with tears. "Anything but that."

The little man nodded, and the walls closed in.

CHAPTER 19

et out," Ingrid snarled.

Sasha blinked, then shuddered: the sensation of something like - but not exactly like - déjà vu passing through her.

"What?" she said - sounding confused but knowing right away that the confusion would do nothing but compound Ingrid's anger, press yet more of her buttons.

"I *said*, get out," Ingrid repeated, her teeth clenched. "I can't even stand to look at you right now."

They weren't moving, Sasha realized - Ingrid's Jeep stopped, if not exactly parked, dead in the center of the dusty road. But then, she reminded herself, hadn't she known that already? She'd been *in* the Jeep the entire time, from the moment they'd left Torrance to the unfortunate departure from Ingrid's parents' ranch that had forced them back out into the desert. She'd *felt* the jolt in her spine when Ingrid had slammed on the brakes, not thirty seconds earlier.

"No," she said, and meant it. Not only because it was crazy, absolutely fucking insane for Ingrid to decide to just throw her out of the car like that in the middle of nowhere - but because she knew, looking out of the window at the stretch of open desert to the left and right and up ahead of them, that she didn't *want* to be out there. That there were things out there right now that might hurt her, if she gave them half a chance.

She couldn't have said *how* she knew, but she knew.

"What the fuck?" Ingrid turned her head ninety degrees, so she was looking straight at Sasha. "This isn't a discussion. I want you out of the fucking car, *now*."

She needed to play this carefully, Sasha thought; to find a way to placate Ingrid without Ingrid feeling like she was *being* placated, at least until they were back in L.A.

"Please," she said, letting her voice soften. "Please, baby. We're in the middle of nowhere here. And I don't want to fight."

"There's a town less than a mile away," Ingrid snapped, not even a little mollified. "Ellacott. It's not big, but there'll be cell signal, and somewhere there to pick up a rental. You can drive yourself back to the city."

Ellacott.

The name *meant* something - Sasha knew it did, knew that she'd heard it somewhere before. And there were other memories mixed up with it, too - not vivid ones, not ones she could easily get at, but *impressions*, the kind she tended to be left with when she woke up in the night from a dream she knew she wouldn't remember in the morning.

Of another town, maybe: one with a different name, a name that made her think of old Westerns and bible classes and the homilies she'd sat through at St. Augustine. Something like *Redemption*, or *Absolution*, or *Salvation*.

And of a woman: blond hair and golden eyes and a colored light around her, her legs tangled up in Sasha's in an unfamiliar bed.

She meant something, too, the same way Ellacott did.

Though what *that* was, Sasha would have to figure out later - once she'd dug her way out of this particular bear pit.

"Please," she tried again. "I really don't want us fighting. And I can't just start walking around on my own, not even for a mile or however far away that place is. It's the desert, baby. There are snakes out here. Coyotes."

"It's a quarter of an hour's walk. I think you'll survive."

She was starting to relent, though; Sasha could tell. Maybe it was the prospect of snakebites, of animal attacks - of being held responsible, should anything happen to Sasha after she'd abandoned her by the side of the road.

"Okay," Sasha said, pressing her advantage. "How about this? It's, what, a two-minute drive to Ellacott? Drop me off there, and I'll make my own way back to the city. Take myself home, and never bother you again."

Ingrid stared at her, seeming to Sasha like she was weighing up her options.

"Alright," she answered eventually - grudgingly, hating herself for giving in. "To Ellacott. *Just* to Ellacott."

Sasha thought again of the strange town, and the blond woman's face, and suppressed a smile.

"Sure," she said. "To Ellacott."

EPILOGUE

Fitzrovia, London, 1933

The last of the guests had left for the night, and the servants with them, when the doorbell rang.

Cognizant of the lack of help, Pearl answered it herself - draping herself in her best silk caftan and the most ostentatiously decorated of her headscarves on her way to the door, lest any returning visitors catch sight of the more quotidian cotton nightgown she wore to bed.

She found, however, upon *opening* the door that it was neither one of the earlier guests nor a forgetful housemaid who waited for her in the hallway, but rather a perfect stranger: a very tall, very thin and very saturnine man she was sure she'd never met before, one whose too-long hair, unkempt beard and somber suit would have put her in mind of Abraham Lincoln, had Lincoln ever been inclined to take a second job as an undertaker.

"Is there a problem?" she asked him, registering as she did so that the man was pulling something from behind his back, something that looked to her - though she must surely have been imagining the resemblance - like a curved bronze sword.

"No," she heard him say, as the blade of the weapon made contact with her throat. "No, not anymore."

ACKNOWLEDGMENTS

've been lucky enough to have a bunch of really great people, in and out of the horror community, supporting me and this book as it's made its way out into the world.

Thanks particularly to E(dward Lorn), Wayne Fenlon, Brad Proctor, Daron Kappauff, Daniel Jervelius, Kev Harrison and Laurel Hightower for their kindness and generosity; to Ross Jeffery, for his amazing illustrations and artwork; and to Mrs Williams, for letting me pester her with questions about everything from cowboy boots to decomposition. I appreciate you all, and I'm extremely grateful to know you.

ABOUT THE AUTHOR

TC PARKER is a writer and researcher based in the fox-ravaged wilds of Leicestershire, where she lives with her family.

The author of the *El Gardener* feminist heist trilogy (*The Debt, The Push* and *The Remembrance*) and the horror novels *Saltblood* and *A Press Of Feathers,* she's been a copywriter, a lecturer and, very briefly, an academic; now she runs a semiotics and cultural insight agency by day and dreams up horror and crime fiction at night, when the kids are asleep.

Visit her online at www.tcparkerwrites.com and follow her on Twitter: @writestc